Dinner at the BRAKE FAST

Dinner at the BRAKE FAST

RENEE BEAUREGARD LUTE

Quill Tree Books
An Imprint of HarperCollinsPublishers

This novel is a work of fiction. Any references to real people, events, establishments, organizations, or locales are intended only to give the fiction a sense of authenticity, and are used fictitiously. All other names, characters and places, and all dialogue and incidents portrayed in this book, are the product of the author's imagination.

Quill Tree Books is an imprint of HarperCollins Publishers.

Dinner at the Brake Fast

Library of Congress Control Number: 2023943953
ISBN 978-0-06-332490-9
Typography by David Curtis
24 25 26 27 28 LBC 5 4 3 2 1
First Edition

This one's for Becky:
my adventure friend, my mom friend,
and one of my favorite people on earth.

Photo courtesy of the author

Renee Beauregard Lute and Becky Sosby
at the Snoqualmie Tunnel entrance

There's no better place to be than under my heavy blue quilt with one eye open when the red Coca-Cola clock on the wall says it's 4:45 a.m. That means I get fifteen more minutes of near sleep, curled up warm in my bed, listening to the gentle rumbling of trucks along Route 202. It's the best. Especially this morning. Today is the day I've been planning since forever, and I get a whole fifteen more minutes to dream about it.

Until Mom knocks softly on my door. I know what it means when she knocks before five o'clock on a Saturday, and it almost deflates me.

She opens my door, and all I can see is an outline of her. She's lit up from behind by the hallway light. I pull myself up on my elbows.

"Good morning, Mom," I say, even though I know it isn't a good morning. She wouldn't be in my doorway before five if it were a good morning.

"Morning, Tacoma. I'm sorry, baby, but I'm really gonna need your help downstairs today."

I don't hear the trucks rumbling along anymore. I don't feel warm in my bed. There's just that feeling, like a dodgeball to the stomach. It steals my breath for a second.

"Yeah, okay. No problem."

"I'll let you get dressed." Mom starts to close the door, then pauses. "He's gonna be fine, baby. It's just one of those days."

I sit up all the way and try to smile, just in case she can see me in the dark of my room. "Yeah, I know," I say.

Mom closes the door.

I swing my legs over the side of my bed and stretch my arms behind my head, my heart heavy in my chest. I do know. But I also know that today is supposed to be my dinner. The dinner I've wanted to make for so long. Mom and Dad finally said, *Yeah, okay, Tacoma, you've asked forty billion times, and we've run out of* nos. *You can make your dinner.* Me and Dad were supposed to go shopping for ingredients today. How can I even mention it when he's feeling bad?

On good Saturday mornings, we wake up early at the Brake Fast Truck Stop. Most of the kids I know get to sleep till whenever they want on Saturdays. But my family runs a truck stop, so we're up long before the sun.

On bad Saturday mornings, we wake up even earlier. If it's a bad Saturday, there's only two of us to run things, instead of three.

I pad off to the bathroom to brush my teeth and roll my hair into a bun. Last year, Hudgie Wilson told me I had "granny hair," and there were a few things I would have really liked to say back to Hudgie Wilson, but I kept my mouth shut. (He smells like provolone cheese, for one.) I have "granny hair" because I cook at my family's truck stop, and no trucker on the planet wants a twelve-year-old girl's long brown hairs in their scrambled eggs. So I wear my hair in a bun.

I pull on a pair of jeans and my Cougs sweatshirt, then slide into my canvas sneakers and walk as softly as I can down the steps to the dining room. If Dad's asleep, I don't want to wake him up by being too loud.

I make my way into the kitchen. "You already start the coffee?" I ask Mom, who is heating up the grill.

"The pot's on, help yourself," she says. "Kettle's on, too."

Kettle's on.

Dad only drinks tea when he's feeling bad. Black tea with milk and honey. Some people drink that when they've got a cold or a flu. When their body doesn't feel good. Dad drinks it when his thoughts don't feel good. He has depression and anxiety, and I guess it's a tea morning.

Steam whistles out of the kettle as I pour my cup of coffee.

"You mind fixing his cup and bringing it to him?" Mom asks. She slaps a chunk of cold butter onto the grill. It makes a *hisssss* sound. That means the grill's hot enough.

"No problem," I say, but my guts kind of ball up in the middle, because it's really hard to see Dad when he's feeling bad.

I pour hot water into a mug and steep an English Breakfast tea bag in it for a couple of minutes, watching the red-brown color curl its way out of the bag and fill the cup. I add milk and honey. Mom nods at me like *Go ahead.*

I head back upstairs, even slower than I came down. When I make it to Mom and Dad's bedroom door, I knock quietly.

"Yeah," Dad says. His voice sounds small, raspy, and far away.

I open the door, and he's wrapped up in his quilt, facing the wall.

"Dad? I have tea. You want me to put it on your nightstand?"

"Yeah," he says again. Small and raspy.

I set the mug down next to a hefty, beat-up paperback copy of Stephen King's *The Stand* and an empty water glass.

Dad rolls over to look at me. My heart lurches. His face is pale, and there's a tear-stained streak across the bridge of his nose from crying on his side.

"Dad," I say. My voice catches in my throat. "Are you—"

"No," he says, reading my mind. "Not so good today." He closes his eyes and a big fat tear rolls out sideways down his cheekbone. "Sorry."

Once I saw a picture of a giant ball of snakes all tangled up with each other in one of those gross-out nature books. That's how my stomach feels now. Like a tangled-up snake ball. "No, Dad. You don't have to be sorry. Mom always says, 'If I don't need to be sorry for having asthma, you don't need to be sorry for having depression.' She says, 'It's bodies and brains, and we're all just doing the best we can.' She's right about that. And you're going to feel better soon. You always do." I keep talking, like my words can fill up the room and make it feel less sad and scary and empty. "You'll feel better soon," I say again.

"Yeah, well." Dad shakes his head, just slightly. "I don't know."

My snake-tangle stomach feels tighter, like somebody grabbed some of the snake-ends and pulled hard. "I know," I say. "*I* know. You're gonna feel better soon."

I try to smile, but it feels like just about the hardest thing in the world. "I'm going to go help Mom, okay? You just get some rest."

“Mm,” Dad barely hums. He rolls over real slow, like his body aches, and he faces the wall again.

“I love you, Dad,” I say, moving toward the door.

“Mm,” Dad hums again.

I leave the room and close the door softly behind me. My eyeballs feel kind of heavy, like there’s a lake of tears that wants to push its way out and flood the whole truck stop, but I won’t let that happen. I hate feeling helpless, but I do, because there’s nothing I can do to help my dad. It’s morning, and it’s just me and Mom today. I blink hard and head downstairs.

The smell of breakfast cooking smacks me in the face. That’s the thing about the Brake Fast Truck Stop. We only serve breakfast. All day long. Breakfast, breakfast, breakfast. I love working at the truck stop, and I love cooking food for people—especially my favorite regulars, who are almost like friends. But if I’m honest, I kind of hate breakfast food.

Actually, I *really* hate breakfast. Eggs or oatmeal or pancakes are all we ever eat around here. You might think you could eat something three times a day every day, but if you actually did it, you’d find out pretty quickly that it isn’t as great as you thought.

It’s the same with North Bend. When you live in one place your whole life and you never leave it, you can get real tired of it. I want to travel the whole United States someday. I want to own a food truck and drive it from Washington to Maine to Florida to California, stopping at all the states in between. My food truck is going to be a dinner-only food truck.

We make breakfast all day long at the Brake Fast because the *sameness* of it is good for business. We know exactly what to buy, and there are never any grocery bill surprises. The customers know what to expect. Breakfast is easy. We can practically cook it with our eyes closed. That's what Mom likes best about it. That's what I like *least* about it.

So I started asking to make dinner. Just one real dinner, for my family and any truckers who happen to walk in. I'd ask about my dinner while I was wiping down tables at night, and I'd ask while I was making pancakes in the morning. I asked for months. Eventually I asked so much that Mom and Dad agreed to my dinner, and that dinner is *today. Tonight.* It's supposed to be meatloaf, green beans, and potatoes. If I'm honest, I'm not all that excited about meatloaf, because meatloaf isn't all that exciting. But it's not breakfast, and that's something.

Dad picked the menu because he's got *his* dad's old meatloaf recipe in his head. When we sat down with a pencil and a half-used-up order pad to plan my dinner, Dad got this funny smile and said his dad's meatloaf was the reason my grandma Jones married him.

"Grandma Jones must have really liked meatloaf," I said.

"I suppose she thought it was fine. But the main thing was, they cooked that meatloaf together right here at the Brake Fast the night she proposed marriage. She said to my dad, 'You know, I wouldn't mind cooking with you the whole rest of my life.'"

Mom walked by just then, when Dad was telling me that story. She swatted him with a dish towel. "And what do you know? Joneses have been cooking here together ever since."

Dad pulled on Mom's towel until she was close enough to lean down and land a kiss on him. "Wouldn't have it any other way," he said.

I liked the sound of *Joneses have been cooking here together ever since.* I liked the idea of making my dinner with Dad.

Dad didn't write down the recipe because he said it was all right there in his head. But how am I supposed to get it *out* of his head when he's feeling the way he is? I need tonight to be as smooth as possible so Mom and Dad will let me do it again. But with Dad upstairs feeling bad, I don't see how it could possibly be smooth.

Then again, when I think about it, *smooth* doesn't always mean the same thing. It depends on the recipe. Sometimes *smooth* is like the creamed potatoes from my *Best Spud Recipes in Idaho* cookbook. Sometimes it's like cold strawberry basil soup from my *Miami Ice: Finest of Florida* cookbook. Other times it's like cheesecake from my *Hey, I'm Cookin' Here: Eating Good in New York* cookbook. I have *got* to make my dinner, and it's got to be smooth. I'm just not sure which kind of smooth yet.

I don't watch a whole lot of TV, because I don't have time. If I'm not at school, I'm working at the Brake Fast. But when I *do* watch TV, I watch Guy Fieri. Mostly, he travels all over the place, eating at different diners. I keep hoping he'll stop at the Brake Fast one of these days, but no such luck. He cooks, too. He says he cooks because he likes to make people happy. I know there's truth there, because number one, Guy Fieri doesn't lie, and number two, I've seen how happy our food can make some of the truckers who come in. If they've had a long stretch on the road without stopping, and it's a cold, late night, you should see the look on their face when they take a bite of our steaming home fries. Or buttery, syrupy pancakes. Or that first snappy, crackly bite of bacon. Sometimes they close their eyes and smile and shake their heads. Our cooking makes them *happy.*

I love when my food makes other people happy. Tonight, I want it to make *me* happy, too. And just maybe I can bring some joy into Dad's hard day. Maybe with some iced cinnamon bread from my *Hello, Dollywood: Treats from Tennessee* cookbook, or else tangy smoked ribs from my *Meat Me in St. Louis* cookbook. I've got to figure something out.

"Tacoma? Did you hear what I said?"

I jolt back to reality in the doorway of the hot kitchen, where Mom is filling muffin tins with the batter we made last night.

"Sorry. What do you need?" I ask.

"I need sweeteners and creamers filled."

I take the box from behind the counter and dip around to the dining room, stuffing handfuls of creamers into little bowls at each table. Then I repeat with the sweeteners—a few white packets, a few yellow, a few pink, and a blue or two. I can't imagine why there are so many different kinds of sweeteners. And *every*body has a preference. One time, a red-haired trucker named Denise waved me down and asked me to refill her table's sweeteners. I looked at her overflowing sweetener dish and then back at her like *Huh?*

"There's no brown. I like the brown packets. The raw sugar."

Raw sugar. Now I'd heard everything. I told Denise we only had the whites, yellows, pinks, and blues, and she said, "Aren't you folks supposed to be healthy-crunchy this part of Washington? You need to get some raw sugar. I don't want any of this processed stuff."

We keep a little box of raw sugar packets in the back now, but just for Denise. Mom says those brown packets cost more than double what any of the other ones do.

"You wanna take a look outside and tell me what we're dealing with this morning?" Mom asks.

I go to the glass door and peer into the parking lot. "We got a yellow day cab—just one driver. I don't know him. We got a box truck with two guys inside—I think one of them is Carl, the guy who doesn't like wheat toast. We got a logging truck with a full load, so the lady driving is gonna want hers quick. And—oh no."

My stomach clenches up.

"What? What's 'oh no'?" Mom hurries over to my side and sees what I saw. "Ah. I see."

There's a shiny red eighteen-wheeler out there, and the driver is the worst person in the whole state of Washington. He opens his door and hops out of the cab and down the steps. It's Crocodile Kyle Glenson, and he's here to make our hard day even worse.

It's 6:00 a.m., and all the drivers line up behind Kyle Glenson at the door.

"Just don't pay him any attention, okay?" Mom looks at me meaningfully. "We don't have to love him, but we do have to serve him. He's here for breakfast like the rest of 'em. Maybe he calls himself Crocodile Kyle, but his teeth aren't so sharp."

"Yeah, I'll try," I say. But my face is already hot. Today was supposed to be my best day. My dinner day. Why is everything going wrong *today*?

"Tell you what. We'll just get Kyle his coffee as quick as we can, and then we'll send him on his way. If we're lucky, he'll come and go as quiet as anybody else."

If we're lucky.

We aren't lucky. Not when it comes to Kyle. Kyle's from North Bend. Everybody knows him, just like they know Dad and the Brake Fast. Except people know Dad and the Brake Fast for being really great parts of our town, and they know Kyle for being an actual butthole.

He bullied Dad all through school, and now he comes in here all the time to eat our breakfast. If he were mean-out-loud to

Mom and Dad, they'd probably kick him right out of the Brake Fast. But he isn't. He's mean in the sneaky way, where they don't *like* him but they'll still make his pancakes.

Mean in the sneaky way is much worse than mean-out-loud, in my opinion. At school, there's a couple of girls in my class, Madison and Piper. They've been in my class since kindergarten, and they've always been mean. But not the kind of mean where a teacher notices and sends them to Principal Henry's office. It's the kind of mean where they pretend all day long that there's a terrible smell.

"Piper, it stinks in here! I can't concentrate on my math!"

"I know, Madison, it's so bad my eyes are watering. It kind of smells like . . ."

"Stinky truck stop bathrooms?"

"Exactly!"

That's the kind of mean they are. The teacher doesn't hear them, but even if she did, how could I prove that they're talking about *me*? That's why mean in the sneaky way is the worst kind of mean. That's why *Kyle* is the worst kind of mean.

Dad has this story he tells our customers. It's about the best night of his whole life. On good days, when things are quiet and we have new customers who haven't heard the story yet, Dad pulls up a chair in the dining room and sits on it backward, resting his arms along the top of the seatback. I sit down every time, too, because I love hearing Dad tell the story.

"Years ago," he always starts, "a long time before my girl Tacoma was born, when *my* dad ran this truck stop, the one and only Bruce Springsteen was on tour with his band. I loved

Bruce Springsteen, and I wanted to go to his concert *so* bad. I used to play bass guitar, and I could play *all* the songs on the *Born in the U.S.A.* album. He was going to play in Tacoma, but I didn't have the money to go. One night, it was raining pretty hard, and a huge bus pulled up to the truck stop. When I tell you the Boss *himself* got out of that bus and walked in here, wet as a dog in a creek. I brought him cup after cup of coffee, and he told me all kinds of stories. It was almost the best night of my life."

The customers always ask, "*Almost?*"

"Almost. After we'd spent all that time talking, Bruce asked me to play a little for him on my bass guitar. So I did. He told me his bass player had sprained his wrist playing cards on the tour bus, and he asked me to relieve him for a song the next night when they played in Tacoma."

At this point the customers' eyes are the size of silver-dollar pancakes, every time.

"And so I did. They took me with them to Tacoma, I played bass on 'Glory Days,' and *that* was the best night of my life. That's why I named Tacoma what I did. After the place where my dreams came true."

Dad used to have a photograph of that night, but then last year, it just went missing. Like somebody stole it right off the dining room wall, leaving nothing but a discolored rectangle and a nail to remind us it was gone. I hate looking at that empty space on the wall.

There's a phrase when you're cooking. *Mise en place.* It means everything should be in its place before you even start cooking.

Measure your ingredients, prepare your pans. Set out your mixing bowls. I *like* when everything's in its place. The dining room's felt wrong to me ever since that picture disappeared.

Kyle's always been sneaky mean to Dad, but it's been worse ever since the picture's been gone. When Kyle overhears Dad telling his story about Bruce Springsteen and Tacoma, he sticks his mean face right in the conversation. Sometimes he claps when Dad finishes, real slow. He usually says something like "*Quite* a story." Even though Kyle's from North Bend, and he's never worked with cows, he has kind of a cowboy accent. When he says it, *quite* sounds like *quaaat. Quaaat a story.* He grins with his gold tooth glinting in the dining room light. "Chuck here tells *quaaat* a story."

When he says things like that, Dad's smile drops right off his face. But it's *sneaky* mean. Kyle's not exactly *saying* Dad's a liar, so Dad can't say anything back like *Get out of my truck stop, you dirty snake.* He just goes back to work.

When Kyle says things like that, my face gets hot and I get kind of shaky. Sometimes I go upstairs to cool down, and when I get back to the dining room, Kyle says something like, "Where you been, Tacoma? My coffee's cold and I need a top-off!" just to remind me that he's still there, sitting in my dining room with his big old gold-toothed smile.

So when I see Kyle first in line at the door at six o'clock sharp, and Dad is already doing really bad, and I don't know how I'm going to make my dinner happen, I get all burned up right away, before Kyle even does anything.

Mom unlocks the door, and everyone files in, saying cheery

hellos, all except Kyle, who smiles his crocodile grin and sits at his usual booth in the corner.

I swipe a cup and one of the steaming pots from the coffee station by the kitchen door, then I make my way to the log lady's booth, knowing she'll want to get back on the road soon. "Hi, ma'am, my name is Tacoma and I'll be serving you today. Can I get you started with some coffee?"

"I'd love a coffee, thanks." The lady looks up at me from her menu. "You said your name's Tacoma? Is that where you're from?"

"No, ma'am." I start to feel heat creep up my face. Because Kyle Glenson is sitting within hearing distance. "I'm from right here in North Bend."

"You gonna tell this gorgeous lady why your name's Tacoma?" Kyle asks from his booth. "Tell her! It's a great story. I'm just sad your daddy ain't around to tell it himself. He sure does tell a *good* story." Kyle flashes his gold incisor at me. I dig my fingernails into the palms of my hands, willing myself not to get teary-eyed. I *hate* Kyle Glenson. I hate his gold tooth and his whole mean smile. "Now where's your daddy at, angel? He doin' okay today?"

"How about *you*, Kyle?" Mom asks, setting down an empty coffee cup in front of Kyle, blocking my view of Kyle's face. "Are *you* doin' okay today? You want some coffee?" Mom doesn't even wait for Kyle to answer. She starts pouring from the pot in her hand.

"Yeah, coffee'll do," says Kyle. "And say, where *is* Chuck? Taking a *mental health* day?" He sneers.

"You might consider taking one of those for yourself, Kyle." Mom sets a roll of silverware down on Kyle's table. "You seem tired."

"Honey?" says the log lady. And I realize I've just been standing there holding a coffeepot.

"Right! Sorry." I fill her cup. "I guess I'm a little distracted today. You want some time to look at our menu?"

"Nah, I'll just have a muffin and this coffee, and then I've got to get back on the road."

"Sure thing. We've got blueberry, cinnamon streusel, and—"

"Tacoma, angel." Kyle's voice gives me the heebie-jeebies. Mom's back in the kitchen, so I have a clear view of Kyle's mean face. The only other sound that creeps me out like Kyle's voice is the sound of a paper towel rubbing across a tooth, which I've only heard once in my life—when Dad tried to help me pull a stubborn loose tooth—and which I've never heard since because the *squeak* of it made me so sick to my stomach that I've never allowed a paper towel near my mouth again.

I turn to look at Kyle. "What do you want?"

Kyle's eyebrows shoot halfway up his forehead. "Now, that's not how your momma and daddy taught you to talk to customers, is it?"

"What do you *want*, Kyle?"

"I'm actually okay with just the coffee," says the log lady. She gives me a thin, uncomfortable smile that looks like *Please take your weird argument away from my table.*

"Sorry, of course." I back away, hot and shaking. I wish Mom or Dad were here in this dining room. Kyle lost us a muffin sale just now, and *that's* a reason to kick him out. Nobody wants to be uncomfortable while they're eating breakfast.

I need to get my thoughts straight, so I head to the kitchen, but Kyle's paper-towel-on-a-tooth voice stops me. It's quiet this time, like he doesn't want anybody else to hear him, only me.

"Shame your daddy ain't down here to tell his big Springsteen story today. I do love hearin' it. I guess I'll just have to look at that picture I got hangin' by my bed instead."

The blood in my veins turns to cold concrete. My vision gets small, and the rest of the diner disappears. All I see is Kyle Glenson, sitting in his booth, slurping his coffee, looking real proud of himself.

"*You* stole my dad's picture." My voice doesn't sound like me. It sounds like somebody in a horror movie who's just realized who the killer is.

Kyle scratches his chin and smiles a slow, nasty smile. I wish his shiny gold tooth would fall right out onto the table. "I don't think you can prove that, angel. Sounds to me like you're just makin' accusations now. You shouldn't do that."

Everything goes red. I can barely see Kyle. If he's still talking, I can't hear him.

"You—you *stole*," I sputter. "From my dad!" My voice is like a radio with a broken volume knob. I know I'm too loud, but I can't turn it down. "You're a *thief*!"

I am only vaguely aware of Mom hurrying over to me from across the dining room. I feel her hands heavy on my shoulders, kind of comforting but mostly steering me quickly and firmly away from Kyle and out of the dining room, into the kitchen.

"He's—Kyle—he took—Mom! Stop! He took Dad's picture—he stole it—"

I can barely get the words out. I'm gulping for air, and everything still looks red.

"Shhh," Mom shushes me. "Honey, you cannot yell at a customer in the middle of the dining room. Not even if the customer's somebody you don't like. Do you understand?"

"*You* don't understand! He stole—Kyle stole—Dad's Bruce Springsteen picture! He told me!"

"Shhh," Mom says again, pulling me into a hug. "Listen, I believe it. I absolutely believe that Kyle would do something like that. But you can't yell at customers in the middle of the dining room. Okay?"

I pull away from the hug. "Why don't you care about this? Kyle stole from us! He stole from *Dad*!"

"Kyle's a turd, yes. But we don't really know what happened to that picture. Maybe Kyle took it, or maybe he's just teasing you. But you need to take a few deep breaths and stop causing a scene. Do you want to go upstairs and cool down for a while? Do some thinking? Because I can manage without you down here for a little bit."

Do some thinking.

An idea sparks in me like an ignitor on our gas range.

I breathe in real slow through my nose.

"Actually," I say, "I do need some time to think. Because tonight's supposed to be my dinner, and Dad's not going to be able to take me shopping, so I need to figure it out."

Mom wrinkles her forehead. "Baby, that's a *lot*. Why don't we wait till your dad's feeling better, and try again then—"

"No." I shake my head. "I want to do this. I *need* to do this. Tonight. You *promised*," I say, knowing that word'll get her.

Mom gives me a good long look, and then lets out a sigh. "Well. I guess I did. Okay, then. I suggest you get busy thinking about bigger and better things than Kyle Glenson."

Mom leaves the kitchen with the coffeepot, and already my vision is clearing up. Already I'm breathing more normally. Already my heart is slowing down. Because I'm going to figure out how to make my dinner all on my own. And I'm going to get that picture back from Kyle while I'm at it.

CHAPTER 3

The hour after Kyle leaves, I'm sure I look like I'm back to my usual business. I pour coffees; I bring out plates of toast, eggs, pancakes, and bacon; and I wipe down tables with a wet cloth. But in my head, I'm planning the most genius heist the Pacific Northwest has ever seen. All I need is Kyle Glenson's home address. Everything's going to work out, because for the first time ever, I've got a reason to disappear from the Brake Fast for a few hours. I need dinner groceries.

I'll ride my bike to a couple different grocery stores—maybe even the Grange for produce—and somewhere in there I'll make a pit stop at Kyle's house. I'll break in, take back my dad's picture, and come home to the Brake Fast to cook the most delicious dinner any of us has ever had. I don't know what it is yet, but I know it isn't meatloaf. Maybe California pizza from my *Golden State of Mind* cookbook, topped with bright green avocados and drizzled with spicy peanut dressing.

If everything goes according to plan, this day might not be so bad after all.

An older trucker named Goose chuckles at me when I fill his coffee cup with decaf for the second time. "You look awful pleased with yourself today, Tacoma Jones. Like the cat that caught the canary!"

I grin at him. "I *feel* like the cat that caught the canary, Goose!"

Pop! Pop!

A loud sound out in the parking lot makes me nearly drop the pot of decaf.

"Now what in the heck was that?" Goose stands up in a hurry, bumping into me. I almost drop the pot *again*.

More parking lot sounds.

Pop! Psssssssssst!

We both hurry over to the front door, quickly followed by Mom and a few other customers.

There's a giant silver flat-nose bus in the lot, smoking from the back.

"How about that," Dad says behind me. I turn fast to see him there, still looking pale and sad. But he's dressed in daytime clothes now, kind of—a blue T-shirt and black sweatpants—which I take as a sign that he's feeling better. At least a little bit. He also spoke in a three-word sentence, which is another good sign.

"Dad! Are you—"

He shakes his head like he knows I was going to ask if he's okay. "No." He isn't looking at me, though. He's looking out the door at the broken-down bus and the choking clouds of blue-gray smoke billowing from the back.

"I'm going to check on them," Mom says. She looks at Dad. "I can handle all of it, Chuck, if you want to go upstairs and—"

"No," Dad says again. "Can't do much today, but I can do a little."

Mom reaches for Dad's hand and squeezes it. It reminds me of how, sometimes, when Dad's having a bad day or a bad couple of days, Mom says, "We stick with him through the hard times, and we love him all the time. That's what we can do."

"Tacoma," Mom says, "why don't you join me out there to see how we can help. Chuck, will you stay with the customers in here?"

I say "Sure" at the same time Dad says "Mm."

The thing about when Dad's feeling really bad is it's hard for him to talk. Once, when he was feeling good, he told me about it. We were having hot chocolate together in front of the TV in Mom and Dad's room. *Diners, Drive-Ins and Dives* was on, and Guy Fieri was eating seafood stew somewhere in California.

"You know how, when you're not feeling good, you don't say much?" I asked Dad, capturing a melting mini marshmallow with my teaspoon. I usually try not to think about the bad days during the good days, but that night I was feeling brave, and I wanted to understand.

Dad looked at me. "Yeah."

"Why is that? Is it like . . . Are you too sad to talk?"

Dad shook his head. "It's bigger than that. It's like . . . There's a wall between me and my words. I can chip away at that wall and get a few words out, but it's a lot of work. And when I'm really low—really depressed like that—I don't have the energy to do very much of that work."

"Oh," I said.

"But hey, you want to know something?" Dad set his mug down on the little table in front of the sofa.

"Sure," I said.

"There's a code to it. I'll help you crack it."

"A code?" I drained my hot chocolate and set my mug down next to Dad's.

"Let's practice. Say I'm not feeling good. You ask me if I'm okay."

"Okay."

"No, you have to ask me."

"Oh, right." I cleared my throat. "Dad, are you okay?"

"Mm."

We both sat in silence for a minute.

"Okay, but what's that code for?" I asked.

"'I'm not doing too great right now, kiddo,'" Dad said. "'But I'll be okay.' Now tell me you love me."

"I love you, Dad."

"Mm. Know what that means?"

"That you love me, too?" I ask.

"'I love you so much, kiddo. So much. Bigger than Washington, bigger than the world.' That's what 'mm' means."

I leaned against Dad's shoulder and he kissed me on top of my head. "I love you that much, too."

Outside in the parking lot, the bus doors open and a woman with long dark hair hops down.

Mom and I hurry out the door and over to the smoking bus.

"Hi there! Bus trouble?" Mom asks.

"What gave it away?" asks the lady. "The smoke or the terrible parking job? Let's give everybody room to clear the bus."

Mom and I both step back. The lady is right about the terrible parking job—she's parked diagonally across three semi spaces.

But I can see why. More blue-gray smoke pours out of the back of the bus, and everybody needs to get out as fast as possible.

A man about my dad's age jumps out of the bus holding two guitar cases.

"You don't need to bring all the instruments," the lady with the long hair tells him. "You need to get yourselves out of the bus! Quickly!" She looks inside the bus. "Denver!"

"We aren't an a cappella group, Nan," says the man. "We're bringing the instruments."

The lady—Nan, I guess—rolls her eyes at him. "Just get out here."

A few other men follow the first man, all holding their own instrument cases. The last man brings out a pair of bongos. "I left my leather jackets," he says sadly to Nan. "Promise they're gonna be okay on the bus?"

"You men have some strange priorities," Nan says. She looks inside the bus again. "Denver Cass, get your butt off of that bus *now*."

"I'm off!" yells a voice inside the bus. "I'm off!" A boy about my age jumps off the bus. He has dark wavy hair that brushes his shoulders, and he's wearing giant, white-rimmed sunglasses. "Could we all take a moment to relax? It's not like the bus is going to blow up!"

As he sees the smoke pouring out of the back of the bus, his face changes, like he's reconsidering that thought.

"Whoa." He slides his sunglasses on top of his head, pulls a camera out of the Nikon camera bag slung across his chest, and begins taking pictures of the bus.

Click.

Nan steps in front of the camera and takes the boy's face in her hands. "You don't know that it's not going to blow up. Unless you're suddenly a mechanic?" She kisses his nose.

"Gross! Okay, Ma. I get it. Everybody's off the bus."

Nan sighs and looks at the bus. "Well, it looks like we're stuck."

"Honestly, it's not a bad place to be stuck, if you've gotta be," Mom says. "Why don't we go inside for coffee, and I'll call a mechanic to come out."

"Sounds good to me," says Nan. "Nan Cass." She sticks out her hand. "I drive this tour bus."

Mom shakes Nan's hand. "Janet Jones! I run the truck stop with my family. A tour bus driver, huh? We've had some pretty major bands come through this truck stop. My husband—he's inside—once met Bruce Springsteen right here at the Brake Fast!"

I'm just glad Kyle Glenson's not here. I look at Nan's son Denver out of the corner of my eye as we walk back inside. He's wearing a black sweater with the white outline of a bear on the front. The bear is wearing the exact same kind of giant, white-rimmed glasses Denver has on his head.

"Whoa," I say. "The bear on your shirt is wearing your same glasses." I point to Denver's sweater, and then to the glasses on top of his head.

Denver slides the glasses back down over his eyes. "I mean, yeah," he says. "That's kind of the point."

I feel heat creep up my neck, and I wish it would go away. Why match your bear if you don't want anybody to comment on it? Maybe he has a bad attitude because his bus broke down. I guess I would, too, if it were my bus.

When we all enter the dining room, I gesture to the tables. "Well, um. Sit wherever you want. Do you drink coffee? I can bring you a cup."

Denver slumps into an empty booth seat, slides his sunglasses back to the top of his head, and raises an eyebrow at me. "I don't drink coffee. I'm thirteen."

"I mean, I'm twelve and *I* drink coffee," I say.

Denver looks at me for a minute. "I'm Denver," he says. Maybe he isn't so bad.

"I'm Tacoma," I say back. "We're both named after cities. Isn't that a weird coincidence?"

Denver shrugs. "You can sit if you want," he says, so I do. Mom says we're not supposed to sit with the customers, but this seems like a special occasion. We don't usually get kids my age, just like we don't usually get broken-down, smoking buses. "Denver *is* a city, obviously, but I'm not named after it. My mom used to drive John Denver's tour bus, and she named me after him."

"Best musician I ever drove," Nan calls from a few tables over.

"Hey!" says the man with two guitars. "We're sitting right here, Nan. We can hear you."

"She's not wrong, though," says another man from the tour bus. He's holding a harmonica, and he blows a handful of notes from "Take Me Home, Country Roads" into it. "She's not wrong."

I see Mom in the kitchen on the phone. She's probably calling a mechanic.

"I should take some orders and get back to work," I say to Denver. "We've got stuff besides coffee. You want an orange juice? Fresh squeezed! Look over the menu and let me know when you're ready." I stand up.

"Wait, you work here?" Denver asks. "Didn't you say you're twelve?"

"Yep. My family runs this place. We live in the apartment upstairs. I guess I'm not officially employed, or anything, but my allowance is good, and I like working with my parents."

Denver whistles. "I wish I had an allowance. Or a job. Or a bed that's not on a bus."

"Oh man, no way. You must get to travel all over the country! That's gotta be amazing." I feel envy swelling in my stomach like one of those pills you drop into water that becomes a dinosaur-shaped sponge. "*I* want to travel all over the country. I've never been anywhere but here."

"I've been everywhere," says Denver, "but it would be nice to stay in one place for a change. Sometimes I spend a week with my grandparents in Oklahoma, but that's all. We're on a bus the whole rest of the time." Denver rolls his eyes. "It's not my favorite."

"Let's watch that tone," Nan calls to Denver.

"See? I spend my life being tone-policed on a bus. Just really not an ideal situation for me."

"How do you go to school?" I ask.

"Online. My mom calls it 'bus schooling.' I've got a teacher and everything, and there are ten other kids in my class. We log on in the morning, we log off in the afternoon, and then we do homework. Same as you, just . . . on a bus. And virtually."

"That's the coolest thing I ever heard of," I say. That dino-shaped sponge of envy in my stomach is practically life-size now. School on the computer would mean no more sneaky mean comments from Madison and Piper. It would mean no Hudgie Wilson dumping salt all over my lunch. When that happened, I came home mad as a wet cougar. Mom had said, "What do we do when somebody dumps salt on our sandwich? We just shake it off, baby. We shake it off." And while I appreciate the idea, in practice, you can't really shake all the salt off your sandwich. It's still going to be a very salty sandwich.

Denver shrugged. "Is your orange juice organic?"

"Denver . . ." Nan warns.

"I'm *asking*, Ma. If you don't *ask* you won't *know*."

"I mean, no. But you probably inhaled a bunch of super-toxic bus smoke a few minutes ago, so I bet nonorganic orange juice isn't going to be the thing that kills you," I say.

"Tacoma!" says Mom. She's off the phone.

"I'm just saying." I shrug.

"Fair. I'll take an orange juice," says Denver.

Mom's forehead has a long crease through it, like she's about to deliver some bad news.

"Ah, Nan," she says to Denver's mom. "The mechanic can't get out here till early tomorrow morning."

"*What?*" says Nan. "What are we gonna do till then? I don't feel okay about letting anybody back on that bus until it stops smoking."

"Stay here!" Mom says. "We're happy to have you. And we're about due for some excitement around here."

I look over at Dad, who is refilling a coffee. He looks tired, and he's not smiling. I'm not sure excitement is what he needs, but I wouldn't complain about a little of it myself. Plus, this means I'll have built-in dinner guests tonight. That's ten people for dinner, even if no truckers stop in.

Mom gestures to the men from the bus. "Those guys might have to sing for their supper, though. Can I ask the name of this band you're all in?"

"Yes, ma'am!" says the man with the two guitars. "We're Nick Jersey and the Hudson Canyon Band!"

Dad looks up from the mug he's filling. "Sorry, you're—did you say Nick Jersey?"

"And the Hudson Canyon Band!" repeats the guy with the guitars.

I've never heard of Nick Jersey and the Hudson Canyon Band, but Mom and Dad clearly have. Mom is fanning her face with a kitchen towel, and Dad isn't smiling, but he's stopped pouring coffee, and his face looks kind of thoughtful.

"How about that," says Dad.

"Can you believe it?" shrieks Mom. "First Bruce Springsteen, then Nick Jersey! What can we get you, Mr. Jersey?" Mom's smiling so big her face is going to hurt. "Chuck, Nick *Jersey*! Right here at the Brake Fast!"

Dad gives an almost-smile and goes back to pouring coffee.

I look at Denver across the booth. I *was* ready to take on today by myself. But it kind of seems like an accomplice broke down right in our parking lot, and I'm not one to let a good thing go to waste. Heists are hard to do alone.

"Denver," I say. "I have an idea."

"Is that idea going to get me unstuck from this truck stop all day?" Denver looks around the dining room with a wrinkled nose. "No offense. It's just really not my vibe."

I *would* take offense, but I'm too busy making a plan.

"I can absolutely get you unstuck from this truck stop all day," I say. "Do you know how to ride a bike?"

CHAPTER 4

"Okay, so you're going to ride bikes to the grocery store, pick up the ingredients for whatever you and Dad planned to make for dinner, and get back here in time to cook it?" Mom looks at me with her eyebrows raised. "You can manage all that?"

"Piece of cake," I say.

"And I'm going to help," says Denver.

"Denver Cass, what do you know about cooking?" asks Nan.

"Um, I know Julia Child," says Denver. "I know Ina Garten. I know that you're supposed to *encourage* your children and not *hinder* them, Ma. And anyway, I meant I'm happy to help with the *shopping* part, not the *cooking* part."

Nan puts her hands up. "No hindering here, I just want to know what your angle is. You aren't usually the volunteering type."

Denver shrugs. "I'm also not the hanging-around-a-truck-stop-somewhere-in-Idaho type."

"We're in Washington," I say.

Denver shrugs again. "Still."

"Well," says Mom.

"Honestly, I'd say let 'em go for it," says Nan. "Denver never gets to hang around with other kids. It'd be good for him to make a friend."

"Mmm," says Denver, with his head cocked to one side. "I'm not really a *friend* person, because I'm literally in a different state every day, but I wouldn't hate an outing. And Tacoma seems very nice. And I really do need to get out of this truck stop. Like, now."

Nan points a finger at Denver. "Be. Nice."

Mom looks at me thoughtfully. "Okay," she says. "Be *safe*. I'll give you some grocery money. Where are you planning to do your shopping?"

"Umm." I think quickly. "The Grange, FreshMart, and . . . probably the butcher on Front Street."

Mom sucks in air through her teeth. "Honey, I don't know about you riding your bike all the way to Front Street. That'll take a while."

That's the whole point, I think. "Yeah, but he has great cuts of meat," I say. "And anyway, Denver's a photographer, and he can take pictures of stuff on the way. He doesn't usually get to do that, 'cause he lives on a bus."

Denver is busy carefully picking a piece of lint off the front of his sweater. "It's true. All I ever get to take pictures of is Nick Jersey and the Hudson Canyon Band, and they are *not* that interesting."

"Hey!" calls the man with two guitars. "*Rude*, kid! People would kill for this kind of access! Someday you're gonna put together a book of photos—*Behind the Scenes with Nick Jersey and the Hudson Canyon Band*. Never-before-seen stuff! It'll be an instant hit. You'll make a million bucks. And you'll have us to thank for it!"

"Yes," says Denver, "I'm sure the whole world wants to see photos of you guys playing Trivial Pursuit in your sweatpants on a tour bus. Really riveting."

"*Rude*," the man says again. "But actually, once the bus stops smoking, somebody should run in and grab some board games."

"How's two hundred?" asks Mom, digging through her wallet.

While I know how to cook, I know a lot less about shopping for ingredients. But two hundred dollars sounds like a lot, so I nod. "Perfect. Thanks, Mom." I take the money she's holding out and stick it deep into my back pocket. "Let's go," I say to Denver.

I wheel the bikes out from behind the truck stop. Mine is green and has a giant basket on the back for supplies. Denver is going to use my dad's bike. It's old and red, and the back tire needs to be pumped up every couple of months. I've just finished explaining my brilliant plan.

"Okay, just so I'm clear—we are committing a literal crime and lying about it to our parents. Is that correct?" Denver polishes his sunglasses on the hem of his sweater. "Because I wasn't actually planning to do a crime today, but honestly, I wasn't planning on our bus breaking down in Montana, either."

"We're in Washington," I say.

"I know." Denver flashes me a smile. "Anyway. I'm open to this unexpected crime moment, and I'm happy to help, but I have boundaries. Like, I'm not going to jail for you. I will flip on you immediately if we're arrested."

"Relax," I say. "Nobody's going to jail."

"Do you even know where this Kyle person lives?"

"Nope. But I know where his nephew lives, and that's where we'll get his address."

Kyle's nephew is Hudgie Wilson, naturally. Meanness must be genetic, because Kyle Glenson and Hudgie Wilson are two peas in a rotten old pod.

"What are you making for dinner, anyway?" Denver asks.

"Dad and I planned on making meatloaf, but today isn't going the way I thought it would, so . . . who knows." Who knows! Mississippi pot roast with Alabama fried green tomatoes? Indiana pork tenderloin sandwiches with Arkansas fried pickles on the side? My first dinner feels a truckload more exciting than it did when Dad and I planned it out. Who *knows* what I'll make. Something exciting. Something memorable. Something that's definitely not meatloaf. "First, we're going to Hudgie's house." Just the thought of going to Hudgie's sends a tiny shiver down my back. *It's for a good cause*, I remind myself. *I'm getting that picture back for the Brake Fast. I'm getting that picture back for Dad.*

We hop on our bikes and Denver follows me a mile down the road. It's late October, and the wind and sun on my face feel good. We ride over the bridge at the gorge, and I yell over to Denver, "They've found, like, thirty bodies down there."

Denver squeezes the brakes and skids his bike to a full stop. "Excuse me, what?" He gets off his bike and leans it against the rail of the bridge.

"Yeah." I jump off my bike and join him, looking down into the rushing water below. "Some of them were accidents, but some were victims of serial killers. We have a lot of local serial killers."

Denver's mouth drops open.

"I mean, not right *now*. But historically. There are a lot of serial killers in Washington."

"Why do you know this?" Denver asks.

I shrug. "I talk to a lot of truckers, and they've got good stories."

"About *serial* killers?"

"About everything. About America. Sometimes about serial killers." I pick up a rock and drop it over the side of the bridge. It's so small and the river is moving so fast that I don't even see it make a splash.

"Like, stuff they've heard on the road?" Denver is looking at me.

"Like, stuff they've *seen* on the road. With their own eyes."

Denver crosses his arms in front of his chest. "Well, first of all, that's terrifying. But now you have to tell me about it. I love a good story."

"Are you sure you can handle it? Some of these stories are pretty scary."

"Yes. I mean, no. But if you can handle it, *I* can handle it," says Denver.

"Okay." I take a deep breath. "About a year ago, we got a trucker in, around seven or eight at night. He was a nice old guy from Wisconsin. Nice but real nervous. His hand shook when he drank his coffee. He told me he always asked his boss not to send him to Washington. 'Anywhere but Washington State,' he said. His boss didn't understand why, but he was okay giving the Washington jobs to other drivers. Then his boss retired, and there was a new guy in charge. 'Please, don't make me go to

Washington State. I'll go anywhere—I'll drive to Alaska—but I can't go back to Washington State.' But that new boss wasn't as understanding as the old boss. He sent the trucker to Washington State. The night that he had coffee at the Brake Fast was his first night back in Washington since 1974. And he was *terrified.*"

"Why?" Denver asks. "Why was he terrified? What happened in 1974?"

"In 1974, the trucker was driving on I-90, just a few miles from here. He saw a man walking down the shoulder of the road. He didn't have a backpack or anything on him, which the trucker thought was kind of strange. He figured he might have had some car trouble. So the trucker pulled over in front of the guy and rolled down his passenger window. He yelled, 'Are you okay, pal? You need a ride somewhere?' And the guy looked up at him and gave this big smile and said, 'Actually, that would be fantastic! Thank you, friend!'"

"Oh my," says Denver.

"Yeah. The seventies were weird like that. So the guy got in the truck and they had a totally pleasant conversation. The trucker told the guy about his family, the guy told the trucker about *his* family, and they just had a great chat. They shared some butterscotch candy, you know, the kind old people like? Then the guy asked the trucker to let him off at a diner in Issaquah, so the trucker did."

Denver cocks his head slightly to the side. "So like . . . That actually doesn't sound scary. That doesn't sound like an event that would make a person stay away from Washington for fifty years. Why would anybody even tell that story?"

"Yeah. It was completely fine. Except a few years later, the trucker stopped at a bar in Minnesota. The TV was on, and it was showing a face he recognized immediately. It was the guy he'd picked up those years earlier in Washington."

"Whoa," says Denver. "What did the guy do?"

"He killed, like, thirty people."

"No way."

"He was Ted Bundy."

". . . I don't know who that is."

"How do you not know who that is? He's a super-famous serial killer from the 1970s."

Denver shrugs. "I'm thirteen. So, if it happened in the seventies, I probably don't know about it. Unless it happened to John Denver, then I definitely know about it, believe me. *Those* are the stories I usually get to hear about. And I don't think he ever killed anybody."

"Well anyway, that's who it was. That's what the trucker told me, and the way his hand was shaking made me believe him."

Denver puts his hands on the bridge rail and takes a deep breath. "Okay, I guess that's a decently scary story. It would have been better if I'd heard of the guy before, though."

"Yeah, I guess so. Anyway, truckers see all kinds of stuff." I swing my leg over my bike. "Ready to get moving?"

"Yeah." Denver gets back on his bike, and we take off again.

We ride past a gas station and an office park. Then a flaking gray house, a green house, and a yellow house. At the end of the road there's a white house with fake spiderwebs stretched across bare bushes in the front yard. Black witches' hats dangle from the eaves, and a big, heavy-looking cauldron sits on the front porch. There's a craggy old broom leaned up against the wall next to the door.

"That's the house," I call back to Denver.

"I love it," Denver yells to me. "It's giving *Hocus Pocus*. It's giving *Halloweentown*. It's giving *Halloweentown II: Kalabar's Revenge*."

We stop in front of the house and leave our bikes on the lawn. Denver takes out his camera and snaps a picture of the house.

I take a deep breath. I've only seen Hudgie's mom at school drop-offs and that one year when she volunteered to be an art docent for our class. Art docents are supposed to come in and talk about a famous artist, and then give the students some art supplies and show them how to make something kind of like what that artist made. When I was in kindergarten, our art docent taught us about Faith Ringgold and her quilted art. All the students painted quilt squares, and the docent sewed them together.

When Hudgie's mom was our docent in the fifth grade, she came in and talked about Edvard Munch and his art series The Scream. I'd seen one of those paintings before, and it freaked me out. But Hudgie's mom told us that The Scream is actually a collection of paintings and prints, and she made us think about the things that made *us* want to scream. Then she had us all scream into a microphone for a really long time, and she said that was our art lesson. She played it back for us, and it was loud and weird, and I am not really excited to see Hudgie's mom again.

But I need to get that picture back.

I walk up the steps to the porch, hearing my own heartbeat in my ears, loud and echoey. Even though I just met Denver Cass practically five minutes ago, his footsteps behind me make me feel a lot better. I knock on the front door.

Nothing happens.

"Her car's here," Denver points out. There's a maroon car in the driveway. The October sun flashes off some kind of glass ball on the dashboard. "Is that a crystal ball on her dash? Wild."

I squint at the ball. "Someone should probably tell her that's super dangerous."

Denver nods. "Ghosts?"

A laugh bursts out of me. "No! Fire. Glass balls shouldn't be near windows, because they can start fires."

Denver lifts his sunglasses. He nods like he's kind of impressed. "Okay, science genius. You'd be, like, valedictorian of bus school."

I grin.

Then the door creaks open in front of us.

Hudgie's mom is wearing a loose black sweatshirt over black leggings. Her hair has a streak of green in the front, and she's got a *lot* of eyeliner on.

"I know you," she says to me. Then she sees Denver. "I don't know *you*." She leans against the doorframe. "What do you want? Candy? Come back on Halloween."

My neck feels kind of hot. "I, uh, no? I mean, I'm just— Is Hudgie home?"

Hudgie's mom breaks into a half smile. "No, I know. I'm just messing with you. Come on in."

I follow her into the house. It's warm inside, and it smells herb-y, like she's cooking with thyme and sage. There's Halloween stuff everywhere. Little wooden witches with their legs dangling off shelves, spiderwebs stretched across doorways, and pumpkins in corners and on every surface. The living room wallpaper is dark green, and the couch is black velvet. She motions for us to sit down.

"Can I get you a tea?" Hudgie's mom asks.

I run my hand over the arm of the couch. It feels like petting a black cat. "No thanks," I say. "Can we just—um—is Hudgie home?"

Hudgie's mom sits down in a wooden chair across from us. "Sorry, no. He's out getting into trouble in an abandoned train tunnel or something like that. You don't do that kind of thing, do you, Tacoma." The way she says it doesn't sound like a question.

"I don't . . . go to abandoned train tunnels?" I ask. The tiny hairs on my arms stand up. Because actually, I did. With my dad. It was last year, and I don't like to think about that tunnel.

"You're a good kid," says Hudgie's mom. "You don't get into trouble. Your parents keep you too busy working at that truck stop to get into trouble." She looks out the window behind me. "Maybe that's where I went wrong. I don't keep him busy enough."

Denver looks at me over the top of his sunglasses. He tilts his head slightly toward the door, like *Let's get out of here.*

"I'm sure that's not . . ." I start to say, looking apologetically at Denver. *We can't go yet.* "Um. I get in trouble sometimes."

Hudgie's mom leans forward with her elbows on her knees. "I don't think you do. How are you doing in school this year?"

"Fine, I guess," I say. "I don't really like school." I don't tell her that's partially because of her son.

"And how about Hudgie? How is *he* doing in school? He doesn't tell me anything."

Oh no.

"Uh, I'm not sure," I say. I clear my throat, trying to buy a few seconds to think. "I mean, I don't know him very well, and—"

"You've been in his class since kindergarten," says Hudgie's mom.

"Right, I know, I mean . . . We're not like . . . I mean, I don't have a bunch of friends or anything, because I mostly just go to school and help out at my parents' truck stop. So, I've never really *talked* talked to Hudgie."

"Of course you have," says Hudgie's mom.

"I'm really just here to ask Hudgie—"

"How is he with the other kids?" asks Hudgie's mom.

Denver's face is frozen in an expression of extreme discomfort. I know exactly how he feels.

Hudgie's mom's face doesn't look as intense right now. It looks kind of *worried*, actually. She looks suddenly pale behind her dark eyeliner.

I bite my lip. I don't want to tell this lady that her son is a bully.

She studies my face for a moment, and then looks down at the carpet. She nods to herself. "That's what I thought. I think he's starting to take after my brother. Spends enough time with him these days, it makes sense he's starting to act like him."

"Is . . . is your brother Kyle?" I ask.

Hudgie's mom looks up at me. "Yeah. Old Crocodile Kyle. How do you know Kyle? From your parents' truck stop?"

I nod.

"Well. Steer clear of him. He's no good," says Hudgie's mom. "But Hudgie sure does look up to him. Spends as much time as he can at Kyle's. I'm not happy with it, but of course I can't take away his uncle. He loves him so much. He goes on those semitruck ride-alongs with him on the weekends—just loves it. An aspiring truck driver. He's going with Kyle this afternoon, when he's done messing around in that tunnel." Hudgie's mom takes a deep breath and lets it out, slowly. "I quit smoking, so . . . I do the deep breathing now."

Denver nods. "That's actually a *lot* healthier for you."

Hudgie's mom glances at him. "I'm sorry, who are you?"

"Um—you said Hudgie spends a lot of time at Kyle's house," I interrupt. "Does Kyle live near here?"

"Yeah, just a few houses over. The crappy gray house with the junk all over the lawn. Never did learn to take care of his things." Hudgie's mom nods toward the window.

Bingo.

"We should probably get going," I say.

"I'll let Hudgie know you kids stopped by," says Hudgie's mom.

"Please do!" says Denver, standing up.

"Now, who are you again?" asks Hudgie's mom, but Denver is already out the front door and down the steps.

I smile sympathetically at Hudgie's mom. It isn't fair that she's surrounded by people like Kyle Glenson and Hudgie Wilson. She doesn't deserve it. "Bye." I wave.

I follow Denver to the lawn, where we pick up our bikes and hop on.

"Wow, that was *deeply* inappropriate," Denver says. "I mean, ma'am, get yourself a friend to *talk* to, you do not need to spill your guts to a twelve-year-old child and some kid you've never even met before."

I shrug. "I dunno. I feel bad for her."

"Onward to the gray house, I assume?" asks Denver.

"You got it."

We ride just a few houses down, and there it is. Gray, peeling, and full of junk. The grass is long and yellow, and there are rusty lawnmowers, rakes, a tiller, and what look like car parts piled high in a corner of the lawn.

"You're the criminal mastermind, so what's the plan?" asks Denver.

"I think we need to knock first, just to make sure he's not home," I say. "I don't think he is—his truck's not here—but I'd hate to find out I'm wrong when we're already in the house."

Denver shivers. "This is a weird little day, Tacoma Jones."

"Tell me about it," I say. "Let's stick our bikes over on the other side of the house. I don't want Hudgie's mom to know we're here, either."

We roll our bikes to the gravelly side of the house and hide them behind an overturned wheelbarrow with no wheel. We cross to the front door, stepping over a few buckets and bowls filled with brown water.

I knock on the door, and then my stomach does a little flip when I realize I wouldn't know what to say if Kyle *did* answer the door. *Sorry, wrong house!* Or maybe *Would you like to buy a magazine subscription?*

Luckily, no one answers. I try the knob, but it's locked.

"Look around for, like, a weird plastic stone or something. Lots of people hide their house keys in random places out front." I stretch up on my toes and slide my hand inside the bottom of his porch light. No key.

Denver steps down and looks around the front lawn. "I mean, it's going to be hard to find a key hidden among all the junk in this yard."

I tug up the corner of Kyle's doormat. It's soggy and says *GO AWAY* on it. What a nice guy.

No key.

I open his rusty milkman box. A silverfish slithers across the bottom. *Gross.*

No key.

I lift up the whole milkman box.

No key.

"Oh. Sweet. Mother. Of. No." Denver's voice is quiet and panicked. When I turn around to look at him, his hands are in the air, and he is backing away from a big concrete planter.

"Did you find a key?" I ask. I hop down the steps and try to look exactly where Denver is looking. There, in the murky bottom of the planter, under inches of green-brown water, is a gold-tone key sparkling in the sunlight. "You *did* find a key!" I hold up my hand for a high five, but Denver does not slap it.

"The planter's too heavy to move. I couldn't tip it over. You would have to stick your hand in that disease-infested water, and then pull the key out, and then try it in the front door, and there's actually a really decent chance that it's not even the right key! That could be a key to anything! No. Tacoma, do not do this thing."

Denver crosses his arms.

"I mean, I'll just wash my hands once we get inside. Relax," I say.

I plunge my hand into the water, which feels bizarrely thick and slimy. I try not to make a face, but Denver has a point. This is disgusting. I scrape up the key and pull it out.

"Let's see if it's the one." I climb the steps again and stick the key in the lock. I turn it one way. There's nothing. I turn it the other way.

Click.

Excitement and nausea wrestle each other in my guts. *I'm getting. Our picture. Back.*

I open the front door.

Holy cow. It *worked.*

"We're in!" I call to Denver.

He follows me inside the house.

"Before you do anything else, please wash your hands." His whole face is wrinkled up in disgust. "I won't be able to think about anything else until you do."

I roll my eyes. "On it."

Kyle's house is small, and all one level. It shouldn't be too hard to find our way around. It's especially not hard to find the bathroom, because there's a wood-burned sign overhead that says *The Crapper.*

"Be right back," I say to Denver.

As I scrub my hands, I hear Denver in the hallway muttering, "Delightful. 'The Crapper.' Why not?"

Kyle's house has a lot of cardboard boxes stacked against walls. There's a card table set up in the kitchen, with just one chair pulled up to it. A dead houseplant sits shriveled on his mantel, and his windows are all so streaky and dusty it's hard to see out of them.

His bedroom is covered in plaid blue wallpaper, peeling at the seams. There are clothes and blankets thrown around on the floor, and there are five different posters of women in bathing suits sitting on sports cars.

But there's no picture of my dad and Bruce Springsteen.

"Crap," I say.

"Are you sure he said it's by his bed?" Denver asks.

"I'm positive. He said, 'I'll just have to look at that picture I got hangin' by my bed instead.'"

Then I realize what he meant, and it feels like an ice cube down my back.

"Crap," I say again.

Denver looks at me suspiciously. "What?"

"He didn't mean the bed in his house. Look around—I bet he's barely ever here. He meant the bed in his truck."

CHAPTER 6

I didn't realize truckers were so forward-thinking about interior design," says Denver as we climb back on our bikes. "They have stoves in there? Little electric fireplaces? Pictures on their walls? They're like a full little apartment?"

"Yep," I say. "Some of 'em."

Denver shakes his head and leans forward on his handlebars. "Amazing. So, where to next? I assume you do need to get those groceries for your big dinner at some point?"

I get a frantic, buzzy kind of warm all over when Denver reminds me of my dinner. Dad's therapist told me that excitement and anxiety can feel like the same thing in your body, so it's easy to confuse them. But this time, I don't think I'm confusing them, I just think I'm both things at the same time. Excited about my dinner, and anxious that I'm going to run out of time. Because there's something I need to do before we get those groceries.

"Yep. But that's not where we're going yet," I say, taking off.

"Wait—then where *are* we going?" yells Denver, following close behind.

"The Snoqualmie Tunnel," I yell back. "It's pretty close, don't worry. That's where Hudgie is."

"Spooky," says Denver. "Should I be scared?"

He's joking, but when he says it—*Should I be scared?*—I'm jolted again, like I've just hit a curb stop. Because the last time I was at the Snoqualmie Tunnel, I was more scared than I've ever been in my entire life.

We turn at a stop sign and ride underneath a canopy of orange and brown trees. They're dropping their leaves haphazardly all over the road, rustling in the wind. We take a right, and then another, past the train tracks, past a farm stand. The closer we get to the tunnel, the louder my heart bangs in my chest. *Think about something else, Tacoma.* I try to think about dinner. *My* dinner. The dinner I'm finally, finally going to get to make. I try to think about hanging that picture back on the wall, putting everything at the Brake Fast back where it belongs. But the memory shards from the last time I biked to the tunnel won't stay out, and I can feel my breath getting faster and more shallow. Why did Hudgie have to be in *this* tunnel?

Dad, that morning before the ride to the tunnel—he seemed fine. Or maybe I wasn't paying close enough attention. There are usually some signs before he's headed into a hard spell, but I didn't see any that morning. I poured coffee, I took orders, I cleaned tables, and I passed Mom and Dad a hundred, maybe two hundred times between the kitchen and the dining room, like I do every other morning. I didn't notice anything. Not even when I reminded Dad about our bike ride that afternoon.

"Sure, kiddo," he said. "I remember. Looking forward to it."

Thinking back on it, though, his sentences were a little shorter than they are on the good days. His face was a little grayer, too, maybe. I should have noticed.

A truck honks as it passes me and Denver. I look up. It's an electric-blue Mack truck—Holden Strawn's. *Blueberry pancakes, sausage, keep that coffee coming.* That's been Holden's order since I was old enough to write it down. Holden waves at me, and I wave back.

"Friend of yours?" Denver yells.

"Yeah," I yell back. My voice sounds strange to me.

The road to the tunnel is too familiar. I used to love the ride, but I don't anymore.

More pieces of that day slice through my head.

I remember Dad that afternoon after we'd hopped off our bikes and locked them onto the bike racks at the tunnel entrance. You can bike the tunnel, but it's so dark that you can't really ride unless you have cycling lights—bright ones, almost like headlights on a car—and our bikes were old, so we didn't.

"Son of a . . . I forgot a flashlight," Dad said.

The way he said it—through his teeth, kind of shaky—made my stomach drop. I looked at him then. His face was different. It was kind of gray and his brown hair was plastered to his forehead with sweat. The lines around his mouth and between his eyebrows were deep. He dug the heel of his hand into his forehead.

"I'm sorry, Tacoma. I messed up. I messed this whole day up. I messed it up for us. I'm sorry."

No, please no. Panic rose in me and tasted like vinegar in my mouth. "No, it's okay! I've got a flashlight. We'll use my flashlight! See? It's totally okay! You didn't mess anything up, Dad. I swear."

A crow screeches from a tree branch above me and Denver, pulling me out of the memory. I feel kind of shaky.

I remember the grounding exercise Dad's therapist taught me when the three of us went in for a family session after the bad weeks last year. I'm supposed to do it when I start to panic or when bad thoughts and memories run through my head on a loop. I'm supposed to break the loop by thinking about five things I see, then five things I hear, then five things I feel. I'm supposed to do it as many times as I need to. Dad's therapist told me that *Apples don't fall far from the tree*, and that the big panic I feel sometimes isn't all that different from the big panic that Dad feels. It shows up differently in us. For me, anxiety makes my breathing feel like a too-hard puzzle. It makes me dizzy. It makes me scared. For Dad, anxiety empties him out for a while, and leaves him with that depression.

Five things.

One. My handlebars. Two. The road, a blur underneath me. Three. The blue sky. Four. The rust-colored leaves up against it. Five. The entrance sign to the trailhead for the tunnel.

"Up there," I yell back to Denver.

We ride through the entrance, past a sign that says *Palouse to Cascades State Park Trail*, and up to the bike rack where Dad and I left our bikes on our last ride here. There are three other bikes already on the rack. I hope one of them is Hudgie's. I feel kind of light-headed and off-balance. I breathe hard through my nose.

One. The wind ruffling the trees. Two. Bird sounds. Three. The click of my bike lock. Four. The crunch of Denver's shoes on the hard ground. Five. My own breath. In and out through my nose.

"Can I get a picture of you in front of the tunnel?" Denver asks.

"Me?" I raise my eyebrows. Denver's question is like a hiccup to my anxiety. A surprise. A quick break. I move my fingers around, because they're numb from clutching the handlebars and riding in the wind.

"Yeah, you." Denver lifts his camera. "It'll be fabulous."

"Is this because, contrary to what you said earlier, you actually *do* want to be friends, and you want to remember this day forever?" I force a cheesy grin at Denver. He rolls his eyes. I wonder if he thinks I seem goofy and normal and fine. I wonder if he can tell that I'm actually fighting back panic.

One. My cold nose. Two. The frigid air coming from the tunnel. Three. Numb hands. Four. The rough wood of the tunnel door against my fingertips. Five. Embarrassment.

"You want me to say 'cheese' or something?" I yell to Denver, who is walking backward, looking at me through his lens.

"No, do whatever you want. I'll take a few and keep the best one," he yells back. He's farther away now, trying to get the whole tunnel entrance in the frame.

I smile. I look down at my sneakers. I look up at the top of the tunnel entrance. I do a jumping jack.

Denver laughs and lowers his camera. "What is happening here?"

"I hate having my picture taken! I never know what to do with my face."

He takes another couple of pictures. Then he looks at the screen. "That's too bad," he says. "'Cause you're mildly photogenic."

I take a dramatic bow. "Thanks." I jam my hands deep into my pockets. "You ready to go in?"

"I'm so ready," says Denver. "Weird little day."

We enter the tunnel.

At first, the tunnel isn't pitch black. At first there's light in front of us, because we're not too far past the entrance. It's light enough to see scratches and spray-painted words on the damp gray walls. It's light enough to see thin, rusty-looking stalactites hanging from the tunnel ceiling like dirty icicles, dripping with what I hope is water. It's light enough to see the solid, paved trail under our feet. Any trace of the old railroad was torn out and replaced a long time ago. It's like this when you get close to the exit, too. You can see in the dimming entrance and exit light for a while, but as you get closer to the middle, there's nothing but dark.

"This isn't so bad," Denver says, walking beside me.

"Just wait," I say.

Another memory shard jabs me.

Dad and I started walking into the tunnel, but I wasn't sure it was such a good idea anymore. The way he looked—the storm clouds of anxiety must have started rolling in during the ride to the tunnel, but I didn't notice because he rode behind me. Then he realized he'd forgotten the flashlight, and it was too much.

We walked in silence for a while, which was unusual for us. Dad and I usually keep up a pretty constant banter. We talk all the time, and sometimes it gives Mom a headache and she does something like sends us on a bike ride. I kept trying.

"See?" I waved my flashlight beam around like a light saber. "All we need is one flashlight. So no worries, Dad."

But Dad was obviously full of worries. I was, too. I wanted to look at his face—see if he was still sweaty and gray—but I'd have to turn the flashlight on him to do that, and I didn't want him to know that I knew something was wrong.

Something was very wrong.

Denver and I are farther in now. There is a fluttering sound by our heads.

"Oh jeez," says Denver. "Bats?"

"Probably not," I say. "Bats sleep during the day. Maybe a bird or a big moth or something."

"This is a creepy place, Tacoma," Denver says. There is admiration in his voice. "I've been a lot of places, and this really might be the creepiest."

"Well, good! This way you'll remember me," I say. "Someday somebody's going to say, 'What's the creepiest place you've ever been?' and you'll tell them all about the abandoned train tunnel you went into with your old friend Tacoma."

"I'm sure I'll remember you either way," Denver says. "'The girl who lived in a truck stop.' 'The girl who made me do a crime with her.'"

"Pssh," I say. "I didn't *make* you do a crime. I don't think we even technically did a crime, did we?"

"We didn't break, but we definitely entered," says Denver.

There is a sound coming from way up ahead. Kind of an echoing laugh. Then someone yelling.

"Hudgie," I say. I'm certain of it.

There is more light all of a sudden, thrown across the wide, empty-feeling tunnel by a strong headlight on a bike, then a *whzzz* sound as the biker rides past us. Bikers love this trail because it's wide and quiet, and because there aren't any cars to worry about. But I prefer noise and cars. The biker is gone in a couple of seconds, and we're in darkness again. Somehow it seems even darker after the brief light.

"Tell me a scary story," says Denver. "You said you had a whole bunch of scary stories you got from truckers."

"I, um . . ." My pulse thumps in my ears. It's hard to think about anything other than that last time in the tunnel with Dad. The memory fills me up like a bloated balloon, ready to burst any second.

I try to steady my breathing. I try the grounding exercise.

One. Darkness. Two. Nothing. I can't see anything else.

"You want me to go first?" Denver asks. "I've got a couple."

I breathe out in relief. "Yeah. Let's hear one."

"Okay. We were back in Oklahoma a few summers ago, visiting my grandparents. Mom and I took my grandad's car to Chili's for lunch. I don't remember why my grandparents weren't there, but I'm glad they weren't. Before we got into the restaurant, the skies were clear, everything was fine. But as we ate our lunch, the restaurant got dark. Not dark like this, but like, eerie dark. Mom said, 'We'd probably better hurry up. There might be a storm coming.' We ate our food, paid, and left. When we got outside, the sky was green."

"Green?"

"Green like moss. Bright green. My mom said, 'Get in the car. Fast as you can.' So I did. She made sure we were both buckled and then she took off. Fastest I'd ever seen her drive. I looked over at her at one point and her face was so pale. Then I turned around and looked behind us, and I saw why. There was a tornado, ripping up the street, coming right for us."

"Oh my God," I say.

"Yeah. I closed my eyes the rest of the ride home. It must've only been a couple of minutes. And then we were in my grandparents' driveway. My mom yelled, 'Get out! We need to get to the basement.' We raced into the house and down into the basement, where my grandparents were already hunkered down. It was the loudest thing I'd ever heard when it passed by the house. It sounded like a train, right on top of us. When we came out an hour later, it had wrecked everything. Torn the screen door right off the hinges. They found it in a neighbor's pool later. It'd shredded my grandparents' garage, smashed the greenhouse, took a neighbor's cat. They never found it. We were so close to being *gone*."

I let out a breath I must have been holding. "Holy crap."

"Yeah. Holy crap."

We walk for a few quiet moments.

"Your turn," says Denver.

I chew on the inside of my cheek. "Okay. I've got one. It happened two years ago."

"Let's hear it."

"It'd been a busy day at the Brake Fast. A lot of customers. Me and Mom and Dad ran around all day, taking orders, making eggs and bacon, trying to make friendly small talk with customers when there wasn't really even time for it. By closing time, we were exhausted. We did the bare minimum—wiped down tables, swept and mopped, prepped the kitchen for the next day—and then we went to bed. But somewhere around midnight, I woke up. There was a sound coming from downstairs."

"Okay, creepy," Denver says. "I'm loving this story already."

"The creepiest. There were footsteps. There was a thumping sound. There was water running. Then there was a cough."

"A cough!"

"So I opened my bedroom door, and Mom and Dad were already in the hallway. Dad was holding a baseball bat. Everybody was scared. Mom held up her finger in front of her mouth like *shhh*, and we crept behind my dad downstairs. There was a light on in the kitchen. Then there was another cough. My dad said, 'We've already called the police,' even though he hadn't. He said, 'So come out with your hands where I can see them.' So the guy screams, we scream, everybody's screaming and it was terrifying. Then out comes old Flynn Marsters, a log truck driver we get at the Brake Fast all the time. He had his hands in the air and everything. He said, 'I'm sorry, Mr. Jones, I musta fallen asleep on the bench after dinner! It's been a long driving week for me. I just got up for a glass of water. Didn't mean to wake anybody!' Everybody laughed, that kind of laugh you do when nothing's really funny, but you're just so relieved that you've gotta laugh, and Dad gave Flynn a blanket and pillow to use for the rest of the night downstairs. But man, it was scary right up until it turned out to be old Flynn."

Denver laughed. "Yeah, I can imagine."

Whzzz. Another bike lights up the tunnel around us, just for a second. Then it's gone.

We walk for another minute in silence. Somehow, the tunnel is scarier when we're *not* telling scary stories.

We keep walking, listening to the echo of our footsteps.

The closer we get to the middle of the tunnel, the further those memory shards dig into my brain.

"Want to hear another story?" Denver asks. "I'd hate to waste this absolute Halloween moment."

"Sure," I say, grateful for the break in silence.

"Okay. This one's not tornado-scary, but. It's from another visit to see my grandparents, last summer," says Denver.

"I didn't know Oklahoma was such a scary place, but okay," I say. "I'm prepared."

Denver takes a deep breath. "There was a group of kids in the neighborhood, and we'd hung out most of my visits for most of my life. Jimmy Spencer was kind of the kid in charge of that group. Well, last summer I hung around them like normal, only it didn't feel like normal. We did all the same stuff—just rode our bikes around town, bought candy at the gas station, and went to the movies and stuff. But last summer they acted really weird. I told them about how the band had done a concert in Boston and on the way to Manchester these two moose got right in front of the bus, and we were stopped for a full hour. They were kind of like, 'Ooookay? Thanks for sharing?'"

I tense. *Thanks for sharing?* I've heard that exact thing before from kids in my class. It makes you feel ashamed, somehow. Right at the beginning of the school year, we had to write about one interesting thing that happened over summer break. I wrote about how Dad took an afternoon off and we drove out to Index to see where they filmed *Harry and the Hendersons*. That's Dad's favorite movie. We had coffee at this little espresso stand that looks right out over Mount Index, and I guess it really *wasn't* all that interesting, but when Dad takes an afternoon off, and we get out of the Brake Fast for a few hours, that's something to write about. Some kids—Madison, Piper, a few others—said exactly that. "Thanks for . . . sharing?" I wanted the linoleum to crack open and swallow me whole. Ashamed is exactly how I felt. It must have been how Denver felt, too.

"So I thought maybe they wanted more exciting stories, or something. I told them about how I got to have dinner with Jon Bon Jovi because he played a benefit concert with the band. I told them about how we got a flat tire in Nashville and the guy who pulled over to help turned out to be Darius Rucker—you know, from Hootie and the Blowfish? And he invited us all back to his house and Nick Jersey and the Hudson Canyon Band recorded a new song with Darius that night, and I got to photograph the whole thing."

"That's amazing," I say, and I mean it.

"Yeah, I thought so, too. But Jimmy and the guys didn't think so. Jimmy said, 'Wow, you must feel pretty special,' which—I mean, I didn't. I was just telling them about stuff I thought they'd want to hear about. About my life, you know? They all seemed really annoyed by me and everything I said. Well, one of my last days there, Jimmy rides over with the other guys. He says they're going to this state park where there's caves and a lake and a bunch of woods, and I can come with them and take pictures if I want. It sounded cool, and I started thinking that maybe I was imagining them being weird that summer. So we get out there, and Jimmy says his family spends a lot of time at that park. He leads the way to the caves and says there's a waterfall nobody really knows about off the trail. I tell him, sure, let's go. But I start getting nervous, because there's really no trail anymore. We were in the woods. After a while, Jimmy announces that we should scatter and, uh, use the bathroom. But there's no bathrooms, obviously, so he means 'Let's separate and go pee behind some trees.' So we do, but then the other guys never come back. It took me a solid fifteen minutes of yelling to realize they'd left me there."

My stomach does a little flip. "Oh no."

"Yeah. At first, I was just annoyed. I tried really hard to remember how to get back to the trail, but I couldn't. I was basically wandering around in the woods, getting more lost every minute. After a while, it started to get darker."

"Oh no!"

"I had a total meltdown. I sat down on a boulder and cried. I started thinking that I was never going to get out of those woods, and that I'd probably die there because bus school doesn't cover things like 'which berries and leaves won't poison you if you eat them.'"

"Real school doesn't cover those things, either," I say.

"So then, finally, it gets dark enough that I see a flickering light way in the distance. I must have been in those woods for at least three hours, but it felt like twice that. I walk toward the light, scraping up my legs in the process, because I don't want to look down—I'm too afraid the light's going to disappear if I do. Eventually, I come out by the lake, where there's a bunch of college students sitting around a fire."

I let out a breath.

"They called my grandparents, and my grandparents picked me up and took me back to their house. But I didn't feel like I was *actually* out of the woods until Ma and the band pulled up a few days later, and I got to leave with them."

Whzzz. Another bike, another split second of light.

"Watch out," the biker calls as he rides past us. I get kind of an eerie feeling. *Watch out.* I don't know if he means *Stay out of my way* or *There's something bad ahead*, but he's gone before I can ask. We're swallowed by darkness again.

"Anyway. That's why I don't do friends," says Denver.

"Those boys weren't friends, though," I say. "Friends wouldn't do something like that."

There's a long silence.

After a minute, Denver clears his throat. "You got another story?" he asks.

I do. An awful one. But I don't want to tell it. It happened right here, and the memory of it floods my mouth with a bitter taste I can't swallow down.

"Uh," I say. "Yeah. I guess I do."

I don't tell that really awful story. I tell a different one. One that still makes me uncomfortable to tell it, like I'm wearing an itchy sweater.

"About a year ago, my dad wasn't doing too well—stomach bug, maybe." It wasn't a stomach bug, but I don't want to tell Denver what it really was. "My mom wanted to sit with him upstairs. We only had one customer that night, and I told Mom I could handle it. His name was Ed and he'd been there so many times before, but usually in the afternoon. I don't think he'd ever been there at night before. He was really nice—close to retirement, always tipped well. He never complained about anything. So Mom and Dad were upstairs, and I brought Ed his dinner. We only make breakfast food, so it was eggs and home fries and bacon, I think. I started cleaning up the kitchen while he ate. Then I hear him talking to somebody. I worry there's a customer in the dining room that I didn't see come in, so I go out there, but it's just Ed. He's talking to himself, kind of bent over his food. I said, 'Ed, are you doing okay?' He looked up at me with just about the meanest face I'd ever seen. He said, 'You trying to poison me?' I was like '*What?* No! Of course not! Is there something wrong with your food?' But he wasn't listening to me. He kept saying it. 'You trying to poison me? You're trying to *poison* me!' I . . . I didn't know what to do. I didn't want to get my mom, because she was upstairs with my dad, and they both had enough on their minds. 'Cause my dad—well, his stomach bug. I kept trying to talk to Ed, almost like I couldn't hear what he was saying to me. He'd say, 'You're *poisoning* me,' and I'd say, 'Those home fries are my favorite, Ed. I like to toss mine with some Cholula.' He'd say, 'You're trying to *poison* me,' and I'd say, 'They're good that way if you like spicy, which I do. I like all kinds of hot sauce, but Cholula is my favorite. I eat it on everything. Eggs, home fries, omelets. It's good on popcorn, and you can mix it up with some sour cream for a French fry dip.' Finally my mom came downstairs."

"Thank goodness," Denver says under his breath.

"Thank goodness. And she saw what was happening. She talked to Ed real sweet, kind of pretending he wasn't saying what he was saying, same as I did. And she called his daughter. We waited with him in the dining room for about an hour, and then his daughter showed up. Her face was all red from crying on the way over. She picked Ed up and brought him home. He went to a nursing home after that, and I never saw him again. Mom said she was really proud of me for how I handled it, though. She said I probably made Ed feel safer by being calm." My throat kind of pinches at the memory.

"So it was . . . He was just old?" Denver asks.

"My mom says it's called 'sundowning.' Sometimes it happens when an older person has Alzheimer's or another kind of dementia. They'll be okay during the day, but when the sun goes down, they can get really confused and upset."

We walk quietly for a minute. I can tell Denver is a little disturbed by "sundowning." I am, too. Once you know about it, it's hard not to think about. I guess I'd always thought that older people with dementia were mostly happy. Maybe they forgot things, or maybe they weren't able to do some of the same stuff they used to, but I liked to think they were mostly happy. But Ed wasn't happy. He was terrified and so angry. I don't think I helped him at all. I wish I could have.

There is the sound of echoey laughter ahead, closer than any of the sounds we've heard since entering the tunnel.

"Since you're, like, an expert on murders in Washington State, have there been any in this tunnel?" asks Denver.

"I'm not an expert on murders in Washington State!" I say. "But no. I don't think there's ever been a murder in here."

"That's good," says Denver. "Because the laughter is kind of freaking me out."

There are muffled voices ahead.

Whzzz. A bike. A light. Then a scream.

Click.

Denver's camera flash lights everything up for a second. All I see is the tunnel. And Denver. And darkness again.

We walk a few more feet.

Click.

"Hey! Who's taking pictures?" a voice yells.

A very familiar voice.

"Hudgie Wilson?" I call.

"Who's asking? Why don't you mind your business?" yells Hudgie.

We take another couple of steps.

Click.

The tunnel is illuminated by Denver's flash again for just a moment, but it's a long-enough moment that I see and recognize all three kids crouched on the ground, their backs against the side of the tunnel.

Hudgie Wilson, Brayden Q., and Carter Bretton.

I expected to see Hudgie. That's why we're in the tunnel in the first place.

Click.

I'm not surprised to see his awful friends Brayden and Carter.

Click.

I *am*, however, surprised to see the giant crate full of something pink.

Click.

SnoBalls. It's a crate full of Hostess SnoBalls. Those bright pink coconut and marshmallow chocolate cake balls with creme filling inside. Wrapped in cellophane, in packs of two.

"Hang on, hang on, I hear another one. You guys get out of the way quick," says another voice. I'm pretty sure this voice belongs to Brayden Q. "Unless you want to get smashed in the face by a SnoBall."

Denver and I duck and hurry to the wall of the tunnel.

A light appears. *Whzzz.* Then *pow.* Hudgie hucks a package of SnoBalls at the bike rider, and he stumbles over the side of his bike.

"What in the— What is *wrong* with you? Why would you do something like that?" He gets back on his bike and straightens it. "You kids get out of here. I'll call the police."

"He'll call the police! Whatever will we doooo?" mocks another voice. Carter Bretton. Carter's dad is a police officer. "Please, mister. Call anybody but the police."

The man shakes his head and rides away. He takes the light in the tunnel with him.

"Call the fire department," calls Hudgie.

"Call the dog catcher," yells Brayden.

"Call the doctor! You might have a coconutty marshmallowy concussion!" yells Carter.

All three kids bust out laughing.

"You're just sitting in here throwing snacks at people on bikes?" Denver asks.

Hudgie, Carter, and Brayden are still laughing, louder now. Howling. The sound echoes through the tunnel.

"That's exactly what we're doing!" says Hudgie. "Want a SnoBall? We've got a whole bunch of 'em."

Pow.

"I mean, *ouch*," says Denver. "That was my *face*. But thank you." There is a crinkling sound as he picks up the SnoBall.

"Where did you guys get a whole crate of SnoBalls, anyway?" I ask.

"Took 'em," says Hudgie.

"Thanks, Uncle Kyle!" says Brayden.

"We love you, Uncle Kyle," says Carter.

"Your uncle Kyle is actually why we're looking for you," I say.

"Ooo, Hudgie, Truck Stop Jones was out *looking* for you," says Carter.

"Shut up," says Hudgie.

I don't say anything for a second.

"I didn't mean *you*, Truck Stop. What *about* my uncle Kyle?" asks Hudgie. His voice is annoyed-sounding.

I take a deep breath. "I know you're going on a ride-along in his truck this afternoon. He stole something from my dad, and I need to get it back. It's really important. It's in his cab, and I need your help."

Hudgie snort-laughs. "I'm sorry, what makes you think I would *ever* help you, Truck Stop?"

Click.

"Stop with the pictures, already!" yells Brayden.

I smile in the dark. *Thanks, Denver.* "The thing is, my friend's got all these pictures of you guys with a crate of SnoBalls from your uncle's truck. So it'd be in your best interest to help me out."

"Are you serious right now?" Hudgie's voice is angry-sulking. "You'd snitch?"

"Hudge," whispers Carter. "If my dad sees those pictures, I'm screwed."

"If your dad sees the pictures, we're *all* screwed," says Brayden.

There's a silence.

"What's to stop us from taking your little camera and smashing it?" asks Brayden, clearly proud of his brilliant strategizing.

"All my pictures are uploaded to the cloud," says Denver. "Smashing my camera will just be more evidence against you."

More silence.

"*Fine.*" There's a *thump* sound, like Hudgie's kicked the crate of SnoBalls. "But just so you know, Truck Stop, I somehow actually think you're more of a grandma dweeb than I did before. And now you've got a grandma dweeb friend, too."

"Okay by me," I say.

I feel Denver lean closer. "Grandmas are a whole mood," he whispers, "so I honestly take it as a compliment. Cardigans and afternoon naps? Absolutely. Those little butterscotch candies? Sign me up. We can be grandmas together. Bridge club all *day*."

I smile in the dark. For somebody who doesn't do *friends*, Denver knows how to be a pretty decent one.

"I'm meeting Uncle Kyle at the Grange in half an hour. You can follow, but don't talk to me. Seriously, the last thing I want to do is spend a Saturday with Truck Stop Jones and—who even *are* you?"

Click.

Denver takes a photo of himself, illuminating both of us for a second.

The Grange. I shiver from the cold of the tunnel and from the really, really good luck I'm about to have. That's where I can find ingredients for my dinner!

"Truck Stop Jones and Funeral Barbie," finishes Hudgie. There's some rustling. "Are you guys coming?"

"With you and *them*?" Carter asks. "No way. Enjoy your afternoon with Truck Stop and Funeral Barbie!"

Carter and Braydon crack up.

"Oh wow, that stuck *really* fast," says Denver.

"Whatever. I don't care. You guys are jerks. Enjoy your Sno-Balls," grumbles Hudgie.

"Kind of seems like you care," says Brayden. He and Carter laugh again.

Hudgie rustles past us, and we follow him back the way we came, toward the tiniest pinprick of light in the heavy darkness.

"Honestly," whispers Denver, "I don't even *mind* Funeral Barbie."

"Shut up," says Hudgie.

As we get closer to the entrance of the tunnel, the pinprick of light widens. It's like a burst of serotonin in our brains—even Hudgie's, it seems like. After a very long silence, he starts talking.

"What did my uncle Kyle take from your dad?" Hudgie asks.

"A picture," I say.

"Oh yeah," says Hudgie, as though he's not surprised. "He does that."

"Steals?" I ask.

"*Collects* things."

"Is that what you did with Kyle's SnoBalls? You were just *collecting*?"

Hudgie shrugs. "Everybody needs a hobby, Truck Stop. Some people collect stuff. Other people bake muffins for truckers."

"That's not my hobby," I say.

"So you and your uncle . . . You hang out and *collect* things a lot?" asks Denver.

Hudgie shrugs. "Sometimes. When Uncle Kyle isn't busy. And sometimes I ride with him on jobs. I get to help him out. He's not so bad, you know. He's a really good uncle."

Something in Hudgie's voice kind of yanks on my heart. It's hard to imagine Kyle being a good uncle, but somehow it isn't hard to imagine Hudgie being a good nephew.

Sunlight floods the entrance to the tunnel, and all three of us close our eyes against it.

"That's painful," I say. But it also feels really good. "Let's get to the Grange once we can use our eyeballs again."

"This must be what it's like to be a vampire," says Denver, blinking. "What's the Grange, exactly?"

We all unlock our bikes.

"It's hopefully where I'm going to get some ingredients for my dinner tonight," I say. "It's like a farm store and a farm stand all in one. It's run by this guy named Hugh who I've known my whole entire life. He's the nicest guy on the planet."

"Hugh sucks," says Hudgie.

I side-eye Hudgie. "What are you talking about?"

"He told my mom I stomped his pumpkins last year."

"Did you?" asks Denver.

"I stomped, like, *two* pumpkins." Hudgie rolls his eyes. "It wasn't a pumpkin massacre or anything. They looked like they'd feel good to stomp."

"Wow, I can't believe he'd be bothered by that," says Denver, looking at me with wide, sarcastic eyes.

"*Did* they feel good to stomp?" I ask.

Hudgie shrugs. "I got pumpkin guts all over my shoes, so."

Denver nods. "A *very* common problem when you're stomping pumpkins."

We hop on our bikes.

"Hey, what did you mean about making dinner tonight?" asks Hudgie. "You work in a breakfast place."

"Tonight it's a dinner place," I say, filling up with that warm feeling all over again. "I'm making my first real dinner."

Denver smiles at me, and the look on his face is very friend-ish, if you ask me. "Live your dreams, girl. I think it's awesome you're doing it."

"Your dream is to make dinner?" Hudgie coughs. "That's sad."

"My *dream* is to run an amazing dinner-only food truck, and to drive it from coast to coast. But I'm literally twelve, so making dinner at the Brake Fast is kind of as good as it gets right now. *Okay?*"

"*Okay,*" Hudgie imitates.

"Let's go." I ride in front of Denver and Hudgie, my heart feeling a little lighter the farther away we get from the tunnel.

The Grange is a little red building flanked by a greenhouse and a chicken coop. Hugh's farmhouse is behind it, big and white and practically swallowed up by yellow-brown weeds. "A pollinators' garden" is what Hugh calls it. It's a lot prettier in the summer. The chickens peck around freely in the yard, and unfortunately, so does Tick Tick, the evilest, most violent rooster I've ever met in my life. Luckily, I don't see Tick Tick this morning.

Denver, Hudgie, and I hop off our bikes and walk them up to the wood railing by the front steps of the red building.

"We can just lean them here," I say.

"Uncle Kyle's not here yet," says Hudgie, nodding toward the empty parking lot.

"This place is kind of adorable," says Denver, watching some of the hens bopping around the grass by our feet. He takes his camera out and crouches down. "I mean, it's not my usual vibe, but it's definitely a vibe."

Click.

One of the hens stops what she's doing and looks right at Denver.

Click. Click.

"It *is* adorable," I say. "I love it here. But you need to watch out for Tick Tick." I kind of whisper his name, because Tick Tick knows it when he hears it, and the last thing I want is for him to come out of wherever he's hiding.

Denver doesn't bother whispering it. "Who's Tick Tick?"

"*Shh,*" Hudgie whispers. "You can't just say his name like that. He's awful."

"He's a rooster," I say. "A really, really vicious rooster."

Denver laughs.

"No, I mean it. We should get inside before he comes out."

"A *rooster*?" Denver asks. "Why's his name Tick Tick, anyway?"

"*Shh!*" I whisper again. "You really need to stop saying his name. They call him that because—"

Tick tick.

The sound scatters goose bumps across my arms. It's the sound of Tick Tick, clicking his beak before he attacks.

"Oh my God, this is gonna be so good," Hudgie says.

"Get inside *now*!" I yell.

But it's too late. Tick Tick comes racing around the building and attacks Denver, tearing at the back of his ankle like a deranged murder bird.

"Aaah!" screams Denver. He tries jumping up the bottom step, but Tick Tick holds on with his giant, piercing beak. A trickle of blood runs down Denver's ankle and into the back of his sneaker. "Oh my God, help!"

"Hugh!" I yell. I grab a broom that's leaning up against the side of the building and try to wedge it between Tick Tick and Denver's ankle.

Hudgie is laughing so hard he is leaning against an outside wall for support.

"Whoa whoa whoa, I'm coming!" Hugh yells from inside. "Don't hurt him! I'm coming!"

He flies out of the building, a blur of yellow and tan, and picks Tick Tick off of Denver's ankle like it's nothing.

"Oh my God," Denver says again, trying not to look at his ankle. "Is there blood? I don't do blood."

I look closer. There's a cut and blood, but it's not immediately clear how much damage was done or whether we should go to a hospital.

"Uh, a little," I say, trying to sound reassuring.

"Oh my God," says Denver again.

"I am *so* sorry about that," says Hugh. He lifts Tick Tick up until he's eye-level, and he makes his voice sterner than I've ever heard it. "That was *so* bad, Tick Tick. That was *not* okay. Do you understand? Do you hear what I'm saying? I'm saying I'm disappointed in you. And you *know* I don't like saying that."

Hugh sighs a disappointed-sounding sigh. He looks at Denver. "Oh boy. I'm really sorry. Let's get you cleaned up. My house is just back here. I've got Band-Aids." He sucks in a breath through his teeth. "Ouch. That looks really painful."

"Yeah," says Denver. "It *is* really painful." He bends his foot back and forth. "I don't think he tore a muscle or anything, but that bird is—"

"Let's get that Band-Aid," I interrupt. Because even though Tick Tick is the worst animal on earth, Hugh loves him. And Hugh's one of the nicest people I know, and I don't want Denver to hurt his feelings. "You coming, Hudgie?"

When I say Hudgie's name, Hugh looks up quickly. His eyes narrow when he sees Hudgie wiping laugh-tears from his eyes.

"I don't have any pumpkins, in case you're back to stomp them," Hugh says. "I'm headed to Cle Elum to pick some up later today though, so come back tomorrow! Make another giant mess. It only took me an hour to clean up the last one."

Hudgie looks like he's trying not to smile. "Sorry about that," he says. "They looked like they'd feel good to stomp."

Hugh pauses for a moment. "Did they?"

"Kind of," says Hudgie.

"Hudgie's with *us* today, Hugh," I say. "I promise he won't stomp anything."

Hugh nods. "Okay. Let's get your friend fixed up. Hudgie, you come, too. I'm not leaving you alone with my inventory."

Denver, Hudgie, and I follow Hugh to his house.

"There's no chance this person is going to murder us, correct?" Denver whispers to me. "You know him, and he hasn't performed any murders? We're not about to get locked in a basement or something? Because my ankle's hurt, so if we have to run for our lives—"

"Hugh's the best," I whisper back. "I've known him my whole life. And he doesn't even have a basement."

Denver nods, satisfied with my answer.

In front of us, Hugh carries Tick Tick in one arm, and Tick Tick just sits there, calm and happy like he didn't just almost murder somebody. We walk up a stone pathway that has clover and dandelions growing between the stones. Yellow clouds of summer sweet leaves and leggy lavender swamp the path, and a giant browning wisteria slumps over the side of Hugh's house. There are bees everywhere. Hugh's whole weedy lawn vibrates with them.

Hugh opens his front door and makes a sweeping gesture with his free arm, like *Welcome to my house.*

We go in. I've known Hugh for a very long time, but I've only been in his house once or twice. There are framed pictures of flowers all over the walls. Not photographs—illustrations. Some of them are labeled, like they're from a botany textbook. His living room is messy and comfortable-looking. There's a braided rug on the floor, a worn brown sofa, and a recliner.

"Take a seat!" Hugh says. "Anywhere you like."

Denver, Hudgie, and I sit down on the sofa.

Hugh disappears for a moment and comes back with a box of Band-Aids and a baby wipe in his free hand. His other hand is still holding Tick Tick firmly against his chest. Hugh's wearing a yellow floral shirt with a tan vest over it. He's got silver-rimmed glasses, a nice face, and scraggly light brown hair that touches his shoulders.

He hands the Band-Aids and wipe to Denver. "Hi, new friend. I'm Hugh, and I'm the owner of this place, and also the owner of Tick Tick. I'm really sorry about that. I mean, I know I've already apologized, but I'm *really* sorry." He makes a sorry kind of face at me, and then narrows his eyes at Hudgie again. "Are you folks here for some eggs?"

"We're good on eggs," I say, "but I do need some ingredients for dinner tonight." I picture the shelves in the Grange, stacked with golden jars of local honey, the giant bins overflowing with squash, turnips, and sweet potatoes, the refrigerators piled high with crunchy celery and bell peppers in every possible bell pepper color.

"*Dinner* dinner? At the Brake Fast?" Hugh whistles. "Man, you've been thinking about that a *long* time."

"Sure have," I say.

"Parents agreed to it? Planets aligned?" Hugh asks.

"A little of both," I say.

He looks at Denver, who is trying to peel apart the Band-Aid wrapper. "And what's *your* name? Don't think I've seen you around before. Are you a school friend of Tacoma's?"

"I'm Denver," says Denver. "Actually, I just met Tacoma this morning. Our tour bus broke down at her truck stop."

"A tour bus! Oh, that's neat. That's really neat."

"Mm-hmm," says Denver, eyeing his ankle with unease. "Um . . ." He glances up at me. "I really don't do blood. I'll throw up. Can you help me out?"

"Well, I don't know," I say. "That seems like something a *friend* would do."

Denver rolls his eyes. "I've been *attacked*, Tacoma. I need medical *attention*. That's not friendship, it's just basic human compassion."

I press the baby wipe on Denver's cut.

"*Ow!*" He startles. I jump. "Do you have peroxide or anything? I don't want to go septic because of a rooster, here."

"Actually, the best thing for a cut is plain old soap and water. That's why I keep baby wipes. They're great for day-to-day household cleaning, too," says Hugh. "Peroxide can actually damage the skin's natural ability to—"

Tick tick.

"Heyyy in there," Hugh whispers into the top of Tick Tick's feathery head. "You're gonna have a time-out in your kennel when we get back outside."

Denver raises an eyebrow. "He has a kennel?"

"Sure," says Hugh. "It's important to give him a safe place to think about what he's done."

"A safe place to *what*?" Denver shifts on the sofa.

I press the Band-Aid to Denver's skin.

"*Ow*," he says again.

"You got any snacks I can have?" Hudgie asks Hugh. "I'm hungry."

"I *sell* snacks in the Grange. You can *buy* them from me," Hugh says, like a teacher speaking to a student. "That's my business model."

Hudgie sighs and crosses his arms.

"I think it's okay," I say to Denver. "I mean, I'm not a doctor, but it looks like he just kind of clipped your skin." I roll up the baby wipe into a ball. "Where's your trash can?" I ask Hugh.

"Just in the kitchen." Hugh nods toward a doorway.

I step into the kitchen with the trash in my hand. It's so green in here—there are big leafy houseplants hanging from hooks on the ceiling, and the windowsill above the sink is crowded with little bottles of water and baby plants with long, white roots. The walls are mint green and the floors are yellow-and-pink linoleum. There's a silver trash can in the corner by the small round table. I step on the pedal and drop the trash inside. Right above the table is a big framed John Denver tour poster.

"Hey," I call to Denver. "Hugh's got a poster for a John Denver concert in Berkeley. Did your mom drive his tour bus for that one?"

"Did your *mom* drive *what*?" Hugh sputters from the living room.

I join them in the living room again. Hugh is sitting on the recliner, leaning way forward with Tick Tick clutched against his chest. "Your *mom*?"

"Yep," says Denver. "That's why she named me Denver."

"Oh my *God*," says Hugh. "Because John Denver was your *dad*?"

"No!" laughs Denver. "But my mom liked John Denver a lot. They were good friends. She drove the tour bus for one of his last tours."

Hugh slides off the recliner and sits on the floor, shaking his head. "This is . . . I don't have words. I'm out of words! My words are gone. What I wouldn't give to talk to your mom. I bet she has some incredible stories."

"I mean, you can just talk to her," says Denver. "The bus broke down at the Brake Fast, so we're there till tomorrow morning. You can stop by if you want. I assure you there is nothing she'd rather talk about."

Hugh wipes a tear from under one of his eyes with his free hand. "I'd like that a lot, Denver. Thank you."

Tick tick.

"This is not the time, Tick Tick," Hugh whispers to the rooster.

Hugh stands up with Tick Tick, who looks like he's falling asleep. "Let's head over to the register and I'll get you checked out with what you need, okay?"

"Thanks," I say.

The four of us leave Hugh's house and walk through his overgrown yard again, back to the Grange.

"Uncle Kyle should be here in a few minutes," Hudgie says in my ear. "You got a plan?"

I nod. "Hudgie, you're gonna get us the picture. It should be right by—"

"No." Hudgie's face turns kind of red. "I can't steal from my uncle Kyle's sleeper cab, Truck Stop. Okay? I can't. The back of his truck is one thing. That stuff doesn't really even belong to him. He doesn't even notice. But I can't go in his bedroom and take his stuff. *You* can do it. I won't tell. But I can't." I swear I almost see tears in Hudgie's eyes. "My uncle Kyle . . . He gets really mad sometimes. I can't steal from his cab. Okay?"

"Okay." I'm not used to seeing any kind of emotion from Hudgie, other than annoyed anger. It throws me for a second. I chew my bottom lip, remembering what his mom said about

Hudgie and Kyle. *Hudgie sure does look up to him . . . He loves him so much.* "New plan, then. You're going to distract him so I can get into the sleeper cab. Denver, you'll be the lookout, so I know when he's coming."

"You want me to *pardon*?" Denver says at the same time Hudgie says "No way!"

I shrug. "I mean, it's a free country, Hudgie. But I'd really hate for Kyle and the police and your mom to see those pictures Denver took in the tunnel. Of you with Kyle's *SnoBalls*."

The redness leaves Hudgie's face until he looks a little gray. I feel bad for blackmailing him, but I also want to get that picture back, and I need Hudgie's help to do it.

"Fine," he mumbles. "I'll distract him. Stop bringing it up, already." Hudgie looks back at Hugh to make sure he's not listening, but Hugh is murmuring something to Tick Tick.

"What's *my* bribe?" Denver asks.

"You don't need a bribe. You're going to do it because you're my friend," I say with a grin.

"Sounds more like I'm your accomplice."

Denver looks away from me, trying to conceal what looks like an almost-smile.

Tick tick.

"Now, knock that off," says Hugh. "I mean it, Tick Tick. Time out. You've gotta do better. You *hurt* somebody. That wasn't cool. It wasn't cool at all."

As soon as we step inside the Grange, my stomach sinks. There are shelves, but they're practically bare. Just chicken feed, livestock-grooming supplies, timothy hay, and some orange mums in pots. The giant bins are only half-full of things that are basically inedible—bundles of silver lunaria branches, cinnamon brooms, and tiny little decorative gourds that aren't good for anything besides decorating front steps. Over by the wall there's a refrigerator with a glass door, and it's packed with cartons of eggs and bottles of pressed carrot-ginger juice, but nothing else. No celery. No peppers.

"No vegetables today, Hugh?" I ask. "No meat, either?"

Hugh shakes his head. "Sorry, Tacoma. End of the season. We've got plenty of eggs, though!"

Crud. We've been gone from the Brake Fast for hours, and we still don't have *any* of the ingredients for dinner. We don't have the photo yet, either. A wave of panic splashes up through me, and I try to talk it down. That's another thing I learned from Dad's therapist. Positive self-talk. When things are kind of overwhelming, I can't think, *Oh jeez, there's no way I'm gonna be able to do this, it's way too much.* That's the surest way to get myself into an anxiety spiral, and if I'm talking to myself like that, it really *will* be too much.

But I can talk the panic down inside my head. *It's not too much. I've got this, and I've got help. I'm gonna get the photo back, and I'm not gonna get caught. And once it's hanging on the wall at the Brake Fast, I'll get cooking. There's time, and I'm capable, and it's all okay.*

Dad's therapist is *very* good. I take a deep breath and let it out slowly.

Over by the register, Hugh ushers Tick Tick into the kennel next to the counter.

"That's quite a setup," Denver says. He bends down to get a picture of Tick Tick in his kennel.

Click.

It really is. The kennel is probably big enough for a Great Dane, and there are all kinds of things inside. An overstuffed dog bed with a bone pattern on it, some kind of swing attached at the top of the kennel, a ball of what looks like shredded paper, a roosting perch, a hanging mirror, and something that looks like a giant spring with dried corncobs inside.

"I like your dog bed," Denver says.

"Actually, it's a chicken bed," I say.

"It's a *rooster* bed. And thank you. He's my best friend," says Hugh. I feel a jolt of sadness over that, but I'm not sure why. Hugh's one of the happiest people on the planet. But still. Having a murder bird as a best friend must be kind of lonely. "Anyway. Sorry I can't help with your dinner, Tacoma." He perks up. "But hey, maybe I'll stop by for it after I get what I need at that pumpkin patch. Man, I'd love to meet John Denver's tour bus driver."

"Well, she'll be there," I say.

There's a rumbling sound, and then I hear treetops jostling and twigs snapping.

"Uncle Kyle!" Hudgie lights up. He's tossing an egg from a crate that's been left out on a stool and catching it in his other hand, over and over.

"Careful with that egg," Hugh says. "I pulled that carton because it's expired." Hudgie ignores him and gives the egg a couple more tosses.

Kyle Glenson's giant red Peterbilt turns off the road to fill up half of Hugh's lot.

"How'm I supposed to distract him, anyway?" Hudgie asks quietly.

"Show him the rooster," I suggest.

Denver shudders.

"Uncle Kyle doesn't want to see some old rooster," Hudgie grumbles. "Nobody does!"

"*Some* people absolutely do," says Hugh, looking scandalized as he walks away from us, presumably to comfort Tick Tick.

"Spill something," Denver says.

"Huh?" Hudgie crinkles up his face.

Denver nods to a shelf labeled *local artisan-made*. It's stocked with pyramids of soaps wrapped up in fancy paper; giant pottery jars full of wooden spoons and spatulas; a basket of colorful, lavender-smelling bean bags; beige candles shaped like rabbits, snails, and bees; and a mountain of bright yellow waffle-knit kitchen towels.

"Genius," I tell Denver.

"No way. Not genius. Not doing it. Figure something else out," says Hudgie. "And hurry up. I don't want Uncle Kyle to leave without me."

I ball my hands into fists at my sides, burning up to the tips of my ears. This is my *chance*. That photo—my dad's photo—is just a parking lot away. If I can't get it back on the wall where it belongs because of Hudgie Wilson of all people—

"Spill something," Denver says again, more assertively this time. He's looking at me. Maybe he can tell that I'm getting heated up. "In his truck. We need a solid, fast solution, and that's it." Denver goes to the refrigerator and takes out a bottle of carrot juice. "How much?" he asks Hugh, who is crouched by Tick Tick's kennel, oblivious to everything going on around him.

"Uh—for you? The kid my rooster maimed? That one's on the house," Hugh says.

Denver nods his thanks. "Much obliged."

He joins us near the door, twists off the cap, and hands the bottle to Hudgie.

"Uncle Kyle is going to kill me!" Hudgie swipes the juice from Denver. "I don't like either of you, just so you know."

"I know," I say. "I know you don't want to do it, but I really appreciate it, Hudgie."

"Yeah, well, I don't appreciate *you*, Truck Stop. I'll get him out of the truck for a minute, but then that's it. You're on your own."

"That's all I need!" I say.

Hudgie stomps out of the Grange and over toward Kyle's truck.

"What's next?" Denver asks.

"We're going to walk toward our bikes, then wait there for a minute, being really casual. When Kyle gets out of his truck, I'm going to jump in through the passenger door, and you just be my lookout. Stay by the bikes, and sneeze really loud or something when Kyle starts walking back to his truck. Got it?"

Denver sighs. "I guess. Let's go."

We walk over to the bikes. I check out my nails. Just as I expected—short and clean. I rock back on my heels. I whistle. I pretend to check my watch, only I'm not wearing a watch, so I really just check a freckle on my wrist.

"You are disastrous at being really casual," says Denver. "Just so you know. This"—he wiggles an index finger in my direction—"is not casual."

I shrug.

A door slams.

"No-good nephew, never did a thing right in your whole gall-darn life!" snarls Kyle, loud enough that even Denver and I can hear him. "*All* over my good leather." He flicks some orange liquid off his hand and into the dusty parking lot. He stalks angrily across the lot and into the Grange.

"Thanks, Hudgie," I whisper.

Then I take off, running as fast and as quietly as I can.

Another truck is pulling into the parking lot, and I nearly slam right into it. The driver blows the air horn angrily. Or at least I imagine it angrily. I turn to see if Kyle noticed, but he must still be inside.

I can't see the driver through the reflection on the windshield, but I mouth *Sorry* anyway, because I can't risk saying it out loud or I might draw even more attention. I am not very good at sneaking. I keep running till I reach the passenger side of Kyle's truck. I open the door, and there's Hudgie. His face is all swollen and wet, and I get kind of a jolt through my whole body when I realize he's crying.

"Whoa! Hudgie, are you okay?" I ask.

"No, Truck Stop, obviously not. Get your picture and get out of my uncle's truck."

Guilt kind of trickles through me. At the Brake Fast, things spill sometimes. We work with a lot of liquids. Sometimes I spill coffee, milk, or orange juice. Accidents happen. But Mom and Dad have never, ever called me *no-good*, or said that I never did anything right.

"Sure," I say to Hudgie. But I wish I could say *Sorry your uncle's such a jerk. Even* you *don't deserve that.* I climb past Hudgie, through the front, carefully avoiding orange puddles of juice, and into the sleeper cab.

Wow. I've seen plenty of sleeper cabs before, but this is by far the nicest one. It's huge! There's bunk beds against the back wall, with a fridge right next to the beds. There's a big TV and a microwave and a fluffy brown bearskin rug. And there's a wall, right behind the beds, just about covered with framed photos. There's a black-and-white photo of a family at the beach; there's a photo of a little kid with pigtails riding a horse; there's a photo of a big city at night, lit up all bright; there's a photo of a Seattle Seahawk giving a thumbs-up next to a guy in a chef hat; there's a photo of a lady who looks a whole lot like Brandi Carlile waving on a fishing boat; and then I see it—hanging right above the bottom bunk. My dad's photo. I step on Kyle's red quilted bedspread and take the photo off the hook it's been hanging on. There's my dad. Holding his bass guitar, back-to-back with Bruce Springsteen. My heart kind of squeezes itself. This photo is coming home where it belongs. I imagine Dad seeing it back on the wall, covering up that discolored spot. I imagine him smiling at me with tears in his eyes, shaking his head, hardly believing it—*Kiddo, I can't believe you got it back for me*—right before I get to the kitchen to cook and serve everybody my dinner. *My* dinner. My wheels start turning again about what should be on the menu tonight.

The passenger's side door opens and closes quickly.

"Wh— Come *on*, you gotta be kidding me," Hudgie sputters.

I freeze. This isn't part of the plan.

Denver jumps into the sleeper cab, a panicked look on his face.

"Hide," Denver whispers, his eyes wild. "*Now.*"

Crap.

We cram ourselves into the hidden cubby of space on top of the lower bunk, right next to the refrigerator, pulling our knees up to our chests.

"What's going on?" I whisper.

"What do you *think* is going on?" Denver hisses at me. "You didn't hear me sneeze *very* loudly. You also didn't hear me say, 'Tacoma! Hey, he's coming. Hey, Tacoma! Hey! Get out of there! Hey!' and now we're about to get kidnapped by somebody who doesn't even know he's kidnapping us!"

The driver's side door opens again, more slowly this time, and Kyle Glenson gets into the driver's seat. He closes the door and throws a pile of waffle-knit kitchen towels at Hudgie.

"Clean your mess," he orders. "And you *better* not be crying about it."

My stomach clenches.

Hudgie sniffles. "I'm not." He wipes juice off the armrests, the dashboard, and the floor space in between the seats.

Kyle starts the truck and things suddenly get very loud in the cab. At least that means Kyle probably can't hear us back here.

I look at the photo in my hands.

"I got the photo," I whisper to Denver. "So, that part's good." I try to smile at Denver, but his face is so stony I stop.

“That’s amazing, Tacoma. Really and truly. But you’re going to be hanging that photo in your *prison* cell, so please excuse me if I’m not ready to throw a party for you, here.”

My stomach balls up, and I remember Denver’s story about those awful kids who abandoned him in the woods. I bite my cheek. He doesn’t trust kids, and it’s because of *those* kids, but it’s also because of kids like *me.* I got him into this in the first place. And I didn’t hear him tell me Kyle was coming. I should have left the door open.

Kyle puts the truck in gear and slowly maneuvers around the parking lot.

“Wow, this day is not ideal,” whispers Denver. “This day is the *least* ideal. Not. Ideal.”

Not ideal is right. Goodbye, Grange. Goodbye, new friend. Goodbye, first-ever dinner at the Brake Fast. Goodbye, all my hopes and dreams. Because if we get caught, I’m never going to be allowed to leave the truck stop again. I squeeze my eyes shut and force my brain to think of something.

Five things.

I open my eyes again.

One. The photo in my hands. Two. The beige walls of Kyle’s sleeper cab. Three. The time on Kyle’s microwave, blinking 12:00. Four. The frowning mouth of the bearskin rug, who looks about as unhappy as Five. Denver.

I got Denver into this, and I need to get us both out of it.

"What do you want me to do with these towels?" Hudgie asks Kyle up front.

"Hold 'em in your lap. Eat 'em. Choke on 'em. I don't care." Kyle doesn't turn his head to look at Hudgie.

"They're soaked," Hudgie mumbles.

"'Scuse me?" Kyle's voice is extra mean now. The way he sometimes gets when he's talking quiet and sneaky just to me at the Brake Fast. "You want to keep talkin'? Keep reminding me that you spilled your juice all over my truck? Because I'll take you home right this second. I already told your mother I don't have time to drag you all over the place."

Heat rises in me, and I feel all kinds of feelings for Hudgie that I usually don't. Compassion, I guess. Embarrassment. Sadness. Still, I want *so* badly for Hudgie to insist on going home. If Kyle drops Hudgie off at his house, Denver and I can get out! I can still get that picture back to the Brake Fast and make dinner and salvage this day!

But Hudgie doesn't say anything. I can't blame him, I guess.

I look at Denver. His face is in his hands, his hair draped over them like curtains.

"I'm sorry," I whisper to him. He doesn't look at me. "I'm so sorry. It's all my fault. I'll get us out of this, okay?"

"How? I would *love* to know how you're planning to get us out of this." Denver keeps anxiously glancing at the front of the cab. Hudgie is just sitting there with a pile of wet towels on his lap. Kyle's messing around with the radio. He lands on a country song.

"I don't know yet, but I'll think of something." I chew on my lip. "He's got a truck full of SnoBalls, and you usually find those in gas stations and grocery stores, right? So he's probably making a bunch of stops today. He's probably going to stop somewhere less than a mile from here. All we've got to do is pay attention and get out the first chance we get."

Denver nods but doesn't look at me. There's a sour taste in my mouth. He meant it when he said he doesn't do friends, and now I understand why.

"I'm sorry," I say again.

"Undoubtedly," Denver says. But he still doesn't look at me.

There's a crackling sound from Kyle's CB radio.

"How 'bout you, Driver?" says a mystery voice. It's a woman's voice.

"Oh, not too bad, not too bad," says Kyle. "Movin' on, and how 'bout you, Driver?"

More crackling.

"Can't complain. Hey, we got a lot of city kitties takin' pictures up ahead, so you're gonna want to be careful. Maybe make a quick flip-flop, take a rest till they clear out."

"What is happening here?" whispers Denver.

"It's like a different language truckers use," I whisper back.

"I don't know all of it. City kitties are police. Taking pictures means they're out trying to catch speeding truckers."

Even though we're in mortal danger, I almost smile remembering all the times Dad and I have talked to each other like truckers. He keeps a CB radio on in the kitchen when he's cooking on good days. He says it's so we can keep up with trucker news, but I think he *actually* means he wants to keep up with the trucker gossip. The radio wasn't on this morning.

"What's your handle, Driver?" asks Kyle. He sounds like he's smiling.

"Raw Sugar, Driver," says the woman.

Kyle shakes his head. "Raw Sugar, ain't that something," he says to himself. He presses the button. "Crocodile, here. Do we know each other, Raw Sugar?"

"I'm sure I'd remember you if we did, Crocodile," says Raw Sugar. "You alone in there?"

Kyle hoots and slaps his knee. "And here I thought I was about to have me a quiet little drive over to Boise. I'm letting my nephew ride along on this one, but he don't say much. You staying on the big road, Raw Sugar? Gonna keep me company?"

My stomach rolls into a little ball. *Boise.* Kyle's driving us all the way to Boise, Idaho. My parents are going to *kill* me.

"*Boise?*" Denver takes a deep breath and shakes his head. "Oh no. No, ma'am. I reject that. I cannot go to Boise today. I will be *so* dead."

I think about reminding him that he thought he was in Idaho just this morning, but I don't. I've done enough to mess up Denver's day already.

"We both will be." I crush my face into my knees.

"Yeah, I'll be here for a while," says Raw Sugar. "Listen, I meant what I said. Just passed a bear in the bushes. Watch yourself, Crocodile."

"A bear in the bushes?" Denver whispers.

"A cop," I say.

"I thought you said city kitties are cops."

"They're cops, too," I say.

"Copy that, Raw Sugar. Thanks for lookin' out. Oh yeah—I see a County Mounty up ahead."

"A County Mounty?" asks Denver.

"Also a cop," I say.

"Why do they have this many names for cops?" Denver asks.

I shrug. "Mice probably have a lot of names for cats."

"Where's home, Raw Sugar?" Kyle asks.

"Spokane. You?" asks Raw Sugar.

"Right here in North Bend," says Kyle.

"Well, hey there, neighbor," says Raw Sugar.

"You spend a lot of time around here?" asks Kyle.

"Sure do. Hey, Kojak with a Kodak up here by the Shell station."

"Kojak with a Kodak?" whispers Denver.

"A cop. With radar," I whisper back.

"You and that nephew of yours have lunch yet, Crocodile?" asks Raw Sugar.

"You ain't shy, Raw Sugar! I did have lunch, but I'm gonna need to pay the water bill after a while, so maybe you and me can meet up at a rest stop. My nephew won't mind waiting in the truck."

"Pay the water bill?" asks Denver.

"Pee," I whisper.

Denver lights up. "We'll be able to get out of here. Before he takes us to Boise!"

I cross my fingers on both hands. "I hope so."

"What's it like, bein' a lady on the road?" asks Kyle.

"What's it like bein' a man on the road?" asks Raw Sugar. "It's all right."

Kyle chuckles. "Right on." He lets out a sigh after a minute. "I'd like to make it to Ellensburg before we meet up, for the sake of my schedule. That okay with you, Raw Sugar?"

Ellensburg. That's not great. It's not as far as Boise, but it's not great.

"Where's Ellensburg?" Denver asks.

"About eighty miles away from North Bend. On the other side of the mountains." I bury my face in my hands.

Denver sighs. "Wonderful."

"Uncle Kyle," Hudgie says up front. "My lap is soaked. Can I please put the wet rags down or throw 'em out the window or something?"

Kyle looks at Hudgie. "Throw 'em out the window? With police all up and down this road? You're not too bright, you know that?" He juts out an elbow and acts like he's going to shove Hudgie with it. We all flinch—me, Denver, and Hudgie.

And then there's a smell. The most vile, putrid odor I've ever smelled wafts up to my nose and gags me.

"Oh my—oh my God," says Denver, cupping his hand over his nose and mouth. "What *is* that?"

I know what it is almost right away. That warm, left-out egg Hudgie was tossing back at the Grange. He couldn't help himself. He must have taken it.

I hold my sleeve over my face. "Hudgie stole an old egg at the Grange. I'm pretty sure."

"*Why?*" Denver leans his face as far back as he can away from Hudgie and the egg, but he can't lean too far because we're smooshed tightly into this cubby next to the refrigerator.

Kyle sniffs. "What in the heck? Is that *you*?" he asks Hudgie.

"No way," says Hudgie.

Kyle presses the button on his CB radio. "You smell that, Raw Sugar? That sewage or something?"

"Uh . . . No, Crocodile. I don't smell anything out here. Maybe you should pull over? Make sure everything's okay with your truck?"

"No, ma'am, that's the fastest way to get a Smokey *all* the way in your business."

"A Smokey?" Denver asks through his sleeve.

"Also a cop," I explain.

"Well, hopefully nothing too serious," says Raw Sugar.

"Hopefully." Kyle tries to smile but the egg smell is getting to him. He wipes his eyes with his sleeve.

"Why, Hudgie," Denver moans.

"Maybe stealing is genetic," I say. I look down at the picture in my hands.

I have to blink a few times, because my eyes are running. The smell is so strong it's like the worst fart in the world that never dissipates. It just hangs there, heavy. A permanent cloud of stench.

"When somebody asks you about the scariest thing that ever happened to you, are you gonna switch out that tornado story for this one?" I ask Denver.

He shakes his head. "The tornado story wasn't the scariest thing that ever happened to me. The abandoned-in-the-woods story wasn't even the scariest thing that ever happened to me."

I wait for Denver to tell me about the scariest thing that happened to him, but he doesn't say anything. Because he doesn't do friends. And even if he did, I wouldn't be one of them. I'm just a girl he met this morning who accidentally got him into a lot of trouble.

I clutch Dad's picture to my chest.

"Hey," Denver whispers after a long silence. "I am glad you got it back. Even if it means being stuck in a stink-cab, getting kidnapped to Boise."

My heart feels a couple of ounces lighter in my chest. "Me too."

Bwoop bwoop.

A very loud sound bursts from behind the truck.

My stomach sinks all the way.

"Aw, c'mon, man," Kyle says under his breath. He throws on his blinker and drags his truck to the shoulder of the road.

"What's that?" Denver asks.

"A city kitty," I say.

Kyle rolls down his window and leans his forehead on his steering wheel. He waits a minute, probably for a police officer to approach the truck.

My body is numb from some combination of panic and being crammed in this cubby for too long.

"You know how fast you were going, Driver?" yells the officer from down on the pavement. "Open your door."

All that talk about cops on the radio and Kyle was still speeding. Sounds about right. I'm barely breathing.

Kyle opens the driver's side door, and the police officer's voice gets closer. He must have stepped up onto the metal cab step. I squeeze my eyes shut as though that's going to keep him from seeing me.

"Driver, you think those speed limit signs apply to everybody but you? You think we— Oh my God. What is that smell?"

I bite my lip. Denver and I are as squished as we can be into the cubby.

"I don't know, Officer. I'm heading to a truck stop in Ellensburg, so I'll poke around and check it out once I get there."

The police officer coughs. "They have air fresheners at that truck stop, son? Because you're going to want to get yourself a handful of 'em." He sounds farther away now. He must have stepped down onto the road! I let out a breath I'd been holding.

"I'll do that, Officer."

"It ain't right. That smell ain't right. You think something died under your hood?"

"I don't know, Officer."

"Well, get that checked out."

The CB radio crackles. "Crocodile, I don't see you. Where'd you disappear to? Hope you made it out of the Smokey Bear trap."

Hudgie fakes a cough and turns down the volume on the CB radio. I get that heart-tug feeling again, because he really *is* a good nephew. And he's got such a bad uncle.

Smokey Bear means cop, I mouth at Denver.

"Sorry about that, Officer," says Kyle. "You know how it is."

"Mm-hmm," says the police officer. His voice is muffled like his hand is in front of his face. "You just slow it down, get out of here, and get that smell looked at."

"Yes, sir, thank you, sir," says Kyle.

Denver and I breathe out a collective sigh of relief.

"That was extremely close," Denver whispers. "I'm pretty sure Hudgie's nasty stolen egg just saved us from being caught. Also, I only thought about this because I nearly peed my pants when the cop was right there, but what happens if we have to, you know, pay the water bill?"

"We hold it, Denver," I say. "That's what happens."

Denver sighs. "Wonderful. Well, if nothing else, this whole thing might convince Ma that I need my own phone."

"I'm not so sure it will, Denver. How would a phone help us right now? Who would we call? What would they do?"

Denver purses his mouth, thinking. "Actually that's a good point. This situation is *bad*."

"Real bad," I agree. My stomach gurgles. I look up quick to make sure Kyle hasn't heard it. He hasn't. "I just realized I haven't eaten since breakfast. I don't even know what time it is now. Two? Three? I'm hungry."

Denver rubs his stomach. "Yeah, me too. I guess that's what a phone would come in handy for."

"For what?" I ask. "A pizza delivery?"

"Yeah. 'We're gonna need you to sneak a pizza to our hiding spot in the sleeper cab of a moving semitruck. While in motion. Don't let the driver catch you. Also, please ignore the smell, thank you so much.'"

We both crack up as quietly as we can.

Kyle turns the volume on the CB radio back up.

"How's your stink, Crocodile?" Raw Sugar asks.

"Still pretty bad, Raw Sugar." Kyle shakes his head. "Worst thing I ever smelled, actually."

"That's too bad, Crocodile. Hang in there!"

Kyle chuckles to himself.

I peek my head out of the cubby just for a second to see where we are. All I see is highway, the gold grass of mid-fall carpeting the sides of the road, and some mountains in the distance. I tuck my chin behind my knees again.

"When do you think our parents are going to call the police?" Denver asks.

I shake my head. "I don't know. Today's an unusual day for us anyway. Normally I work all day Saturday at the truck stop. But you're here, and we're supposed to be shopping for groceries . . . I don't know what time I'm supposed to be back."

"Yeah, it's a weird day for me, too. My mom's probably just glad I've got a *friend* to hang out with while she's dealing with the broken-down bus, so I don't know that she's expecting me back anytime soon." Denver makes air quotes with his fingers when he says the word *friend*. *I've got a friend to hang out with.* Even with the air quotes, my heart feels kind of cozy all of a sudden, like it's wearing a little sweater. Drinking a little cup of cocoa. Reading a little book in front of a little fire.

I don't really have friends. I've got truckers who I like to talk to, and truckers who I don't like to talk to. But the kids in my class are like aliens to me. Or maybe *I'm* the alien. They hang out at each other's houses, and talk about sleepovers and funny internet videos, and whose parent is driving which kids where. They use their phones all the time. *All* the time. They don't have jobs. Most of them have never been to a truck stop. Never even met a trucker. I don't have a single thing in common with any of them.

Unlike Denver, I really want a friend.

We sit in silence for a long while. Every so often, Kyle's CB radio crackles to life. Sometimes it's other truckers. Mostly it's Raw Sugar.

"'Bout ten miles from Ellensburg, Crocodile. We still on for a meet-cute?"

Kyle hoots. "Abso*lute*ly, ma'am! I sure am." He tugs the collar of his shirt up to his nose and sniffs. He shrugs.

By now, the stink is a part of all of us. I can still smell it, but it smells normal. Like everything will always be the stink. The smell is on all four of us—me, Denver, Hudgie, and Kyle—and it's on everything in the cab, too. I wonder if Raw Sugar will mind the stink when she meets Kyle. Maybe it will distract her long enough for me and Denver to sneak out of the cab. We'll go right inside, ask the people running the truck stop to use their phone, and get some food. It'll be okay. We'll be in a whole world of trouble, but we'll be alive and not in Idaho. We've just gotta get out of this truck.

"Ten miles," I whisper to Denver. It feels like we've been driving forever. My whole body hurts from being jammed into the cubby.

Denver lets out a relieved sigh. "That's good, because I really need to pee. I didn't want to tell you how dire the situation is, but. It's dire, Tacoma."

"Gross," I whisper. "Hold it till we get there."

"I'll try."

I try to wiggle myself a little farther away from Denver, but I'm up against the wall as it is. *Please don't pee, Denver Cass.*

"You're gonna see a sign for Olive's Juice-Up in a couple of minutes," says Raw Sugar. "Tiny little stop, but they make a good cup of coffee."

"Sounds good, Raw Sugar," says Kyle. "Hey, how'm I gonna know it's you when I see you?"

"I'm wearing a Seahawks jacket and I've got long red hair," says Raw Sugar.

"Shoot! Long red hair," Kyle says to himself. "Kyle, you lucky dog."

"Gross," I whisper to Denver.

"Very gross," Denver agrees.

"I hope Raw Sugar realizes he's a creep by the time their coffee comes. She's about to save our butts."

Denver holds up his crossed fingers. "I hope so."

I peek out from the cubby and look out the windshield. There's a road sign shaped like a big green olive. It says *Olive's Juice-Up* in giant orange letters. Right under the sign is a little parking lot for big trucks, and a tiny little brick building.

"Crap," I whisper.

"What's the matter?" Denver asks.

"This stop is tiny, Denver. There's no way we're going to be able to go inside without Kyle seeing us."

"I think the first thing to do is to get out of the truck. If we have to hide behind the building while he finishes his date, then that's what we have to do. We just need to get out of the truck."

Kyle pulls the truck into one of the parking spots at Olive's Juice-Up. There's two other semis in the lot. I assume one of them belongs to Raw Sugar.

Kyle shuts off the truck and unbuckles his seatbelt. Hudgie unbuckles, too.

"Where'd you think you're going?" Kyle asks him.

"It stinks in here! And you can't just leave me in the truck. My mom said—"

"Your mom says a lot of things. You'd be smart not to listen to most of 'em. I sure don't. You're staying in the truck."

Hudgie slumps down in his seat.

"Be good out here 'n maybe I'll bring you something to eat when I'm done."

Hudgie doesn't say anything.

"Stop pouting. You look like a fool and a baby." Kyle gets out of the cab and slams the door behind him.

Denver and I both breathe out noisily in relief. "Oh man, I can't wait to get out of here," Denver says.

I hand him my dad's photo. My fingers are stiff from clutching the frame for so long. "Can you put this in your camera bag?" I ask.

He unzips his bag, hangs his camera around his neck, and carefully fits the photo inside the case. I keep my head low as I watch Kyle open the front door of the building and walk inside.

"Let's go!" I hop off the bottom bunk and nearly fall over. "Ow!"

"Yeah, my legs are asleep too," says Denver.

"I'm coming with you guys," says Hudgie quietly. He's turned around, looking right at us.

Denver and I freeze.

"What?" I say, even though I heard him.

"I'm coming with you. I don't want to stay here with him. He's a jerk." Hudgie blinks hard, like he's trying to keep from crying again. "You heard him. He treats me like crap."

Hudgie's voice sounds kind of wobbly. Maybe this is the first time Kyle's treated Hudgie like that in front of other people, even if Kyle didn't know it. Maybe now it's harder for Hudgie to pretend his uncle isn't so bad.

"Well, Tacoma's the boss, so . . ." Denver looks at me.

"He does treat you like crap," I say. "I'm really sorry about that, Hudgie. I wouldn't want to be stuck with Kyle, either. Come on." I stomp my feet to wake up my legs. I wince at the sharp needle-y feeling in my calves. "But we need to get out of here before he comes back. What's he going to do when he sees that you're missing?"

"Nothing," says Hudgie. "Be glad he doesn't have to bring me all the way to Boise after all, I guess."

"So we leave," says Denver. "All three of us. And then what?"

"And then . . . I guess we wait for Kyle to get out of here, and we go inside and ask to use a phone."

"If either of you grandmas ever says a word about anything you heard in this truck, I'll feed you to that rabid rooster," growls Hudgie.

Denver and I both nod.

"Tacoma," says Denver, "I can't wait for Kyle to leave. I need to use a bathroom. A bathroom with a sink where I can attempt to wash the egg-stink from the truck off of me. And I need something to eat."

"Me too," I agree.

"Me three," echoes Hudgie.

Denver finally stands up. Hudgie puts a hand on the door handle.

"Hang on, Hudgie. Did you steal an egg from the Grange?"

Hudgie's face clouds over. "I mean, it was sitting out. Nobody was gonna buy a carton of old warm eggs. I thought it'd be funny if I hid it in a mailbox or something. Why, are you gonna rat me out?"

"Not for this. I mean, you should work on the stealing thing, but you're right. Nobody'd want that old egg. Why don't you leave your sweatshirt behind so we don't have to smell it for the rest of the day?"

"And so Uncle Kyle does," Hudgie says, reading my mind. He half smiles. "Yeah, okay."

He unzips his sweatshirt and adds it to the pile of wet towels on the floor. Then we both spot the Post-it pad stuffed into the dashboard at the same time.

Hudgie opens the glove box and finds a pen. He dislodges the Post-it pad and scrawls:

FOUND A RIDE HOME, JUNKLE KYLE. ENJOY YOUR DATE.

He sticks the note to the windshield.

"Junkle Kyle," I say. "That's your best work yet."

"Thanks, Truck Stop," says Hudgie, opening the door and jumping to the ground.

"I'm fond of Funeral Barbie, myself," says Denver before slamming the door. "I hope I never see you again, big truck."

I scan the area. There isn't much. There's Olive's, obviously. And there's the road. There's a building in the distance down the interstate, but I can't tell what it is.

"Want to walk that way?" I ask. "See if somebody in that building can help us? Use their bathroom?"

"It's better than the alternative," says Denver. "Let's go."

The three of us start walking down the shoulder of the road.

A green car honks at us as it passes.

"This isn't how I thought today was going to go," says Denver.

I cross my legs tight because I am probably closer to peeing my pants than I've been since I was about four years old. I kind of crouch down for a second.

"Tell me about it," I say.

I can stand up again. We waddle in silence for a minute.

"Is it just me, or is that building not actually getting any closer?" says Denver. "It's like a mirage in the desert."

I squint. He's right. "Yeah. Except we're not dying of thirst. We just *really* have to pee."

It feels like we're moving down the road for half a mile. Finally we're there—in front of a long brick building with a cracked black sign out front. *Ellensburg Curiosities and Oddities Mall.*

"Mm," says Denver, "this is definitely bad news, right? But even worse news is that I literally can't wait another second. I need a bathroom *now.*"

I take a deep breath.

This place looks scary, and I'm not sure why. Maybe it's the name. *Curiosities and Oddities.* Maybe it's the worn-down look of the building. Maybe it's the stack of human skulls behind the iron-barred front window.

"Do you think those are real?" I ask.

"Definitely," says Hudgie.

"I choose not to think about it," hisses Denver. "Let's go in. If losing my head is the price I have to pay *not* to pee my pants, so be it."

We walk up to the door and I pull it open. There's a sign right on the wall in front of us that says *Restrooms*, with an arrow pointing to the right. Denver, Hudgie, and I practically speed-walk to the bathrooms.

When we're all finished, we meet up again right outside the bathroom doors.

"Okay. What next?" Denver asks. "Maybe we can find someone who'll let us use their phone?"

I sigh. "Yeah, good idea." I want to get rescued from Ellensburg, but calling my parents means I'm going to have to tell them about sneaking into Kyle's truck, and I am not prepared for that amount of trouble. I practically never get in trouble. How much trouble can you get into cooking eggs? I don't even know what trouble looks like at the Brake Fast. Dad's having a really bad day, and this isn't going to help. And there's no *way* Mom and Dad are going to let me cook dinner tonight after they find out about everything.

We walk slowly to the desk at the other end of the long, eerie shop. It really is a little like a mall, except instead of clothing stores, there's a booth of dried-out bats with leathery wings attached to wooden plaques. Instead of a food court, there's a long wooden table with little jam jars of bugs. The sign above the table says *Edible insects, $7 a jar. Protein! Tasty! Scare your friends!* I squint at a jar. There are crickets in there, grasshoppers, and some kind of worm.

"Gross," I say under my breath.

Hudgie reaches out for one of the jars.

"Don't even think about stealing that," warns Denver.

Hudgie pulls his hand back.

And instead of the guy at the mall kiosk who clacks his hair straightener or flies a drone at you as you walk by, there's a very tiny old woman at the checkout counter at the far end of the store. Her hair is whitish purple, and she is wearing black lace gloves that look like spiderwebs. "Well, well." Her voice is like a jar of old rusty nails. She sounds like an actual witch. I wonder if we accidentally stumbled into a witch's house and remember that it usually doesn't end well for children. "Who do we have here at our little shop?"

"Um, hi, ma'am." I take a deep breath and try to be brave. "My name is Tacoma Jones, and this is Denver and Hudgie."

Denver gives a little wave. Hudgie tries to smile but looks kind of terrified.

"Those are strange names," accuses the little old woman. She turns around to the giant black leather purse hung across the chair behind her. She rifles through it with her tiny hands until she finds a lipstick.

"This is a strange shop," I say back, feeling a little braver and kind of annoyed about the name comment.

"Thank you," says the little old woman. She takes the lid off the lipstick and swipes it across her mouth. It's an odd shade of lilac. "What are you looking for, girl? Perfume? I think you could use a nice perfume." She waves her hand in front of her nose.

I'm offended for a moment before I remember that we all probably still smell like a bag of rotten eggs. It's amazing how easily you get used to a smell.

"Uh, no, thanks. Actually, do you have a phone we can use? We're kind of far from home, and we need a ride back."

"I have *endless* phones you can use, my dear girl." The old woman grins at me, and her teeth are kind of yellow and very small.

"Great, thanks," I say.

"Follow the telephone sign." She waves her hand toward a sign with a picture of an old-fashioned telephone and an arrow on it.

"Um, okay." I glance at Denver and Hudgie. "Let's go."

We wind around racks of old, stained clothing.

"Ew," says Denver. "Is that blood?"

"Probably," I say. "Let's just call home and get out of here."

Click.

Denver snaps a photo of the clothes.

There is a wide glass case against a wall. It's full of clear boxes of hair—human hair, in every shade I can think of—all stacked up like a pyramid. The boxes are labeled.

"Lucille Ball," reads Denver. "Keanu Reeves, Zooey Deschanel, John Stamos."

"I guess everybody has a hobby," I say. "Do you collect anything?"

"I collect everything," says Hudgie. "Mostly stuff I can fit in my pocket."

Denver rolls his eyes. "The stealing, Hudgie. I can't."

"Well," I say, "I collect cookbooks from different states, but now I'm thinking I should get started on my human hair collection."

Denver grins. "Gross. The cookbooks sound cool, though."

"They are! I've got a bunch. They've taught me a lot about cooking, even though I'm kind of destined to cook the same meals over and over again, at least for the near future."

"Eggs." Hudgie nods.

"Eggs. Pancakes. But someday I'm going to make Maine lobster from my *Maine Course* cookbook. And pralines from my *Sweet Carolina* cookbook. And a Juicy Lucy cheeseburger from my *Ope, A Minnesota Menu* cookbook. I'll make all of it. I've read those cookbooks cover to cover so many times that I've practically memorized them."

"I'd eat all of that," says Denver. "All that stuff. Delish. Let me know when your food truck is up and running. I'll be your best customer."

I get kind of a warm feeling in my stomach. "I will," I say.

"I wish you could make that stuff tonight," Hudgie says, rubbing his stomach.

"Me too." I half smile at Hudgie, and realize this is the only kind-of-nice conversation we've ever had. And I've known him since kindergarten.

We dodge tables of tools that look like they could be used in the kitchen or in an old, unsanitary hospital, or maybe an auto garage. There is a giant shelf of taxidermy animals wearing clothing—dead cats wearing top hats and long coats, a baby raccoon wearing a bonnet and clutching a rattle in her claws, a whole flock of birds wearing tiny high-heeled shoes—and a table of the creepiest old dolls I have ever seen in my life. I hate creepy old dolls.

Bang. Clink.

Denver's eyes get huge. "What was that?"

"No idea," I say. "But it's definitely something bad, right?" I try to laugh, but no sound comes out.

"If I die in here, I want you to have my camera," whispers Denver.

"Who?" says Hudgie, looking up from stuffing a ratty doll wig into his jeans pocket. "Me or her?"

"Her," says Denver. "Put the doll wig back, you weirdo. It's like you *want* to get haunted."

"*You're* a weirdo," says Hudgie, grudgingly pulling the wig out of his pocket and replacing it crookedly on the bald head of a cracked-face doll.

"Let's just find the phones and go wait outside for our ride," I whisper.

Denver nods.

There's another telephone sign with an arrow pointing right, down a dusty hallway lined with glass cases full of crystals. We follow the sign, but the second we step out of the hallway, my stomach sinks.

"No way," says Denver.

There is a huge case of old telephones. The kind where you stick your finger inside the number slots and rotate the wheel. The kind where the listening part is separate from the talking part, so you have to pick up the listening part and hold it to your ear while you yell into the other part. I've seen them in old movies. There's even an entire phone booth next to the case, covered in graffiti. And of course, none of these phones are connected to anything.

"Well, perfect. I guess we live here now." I rest my forehead in my hand.

Click.

Denver lowers his camera.

"It was probably that lady's idea of a joke. Let's go back to the desk and ask to use her *real* phone."

We do go back to the desk. Past the crystals and the creepy dolls and the taxidermy animals and the stained clothes. Back to where we saw the old lady with the rusty-nails voice. Only, the lady isn't there. No one is.

"Ma'am?" I say. My voice quivers a little. "Excuse me?"

"Maybe she went outside to smoke," suggests Hudgie.

We walk through the main area between the desk and the front door. I grab onto the handle and pull, but nothing happens. I pull as hard as I can with my entire body weight. Nothing. "Oh my God. Did she leave and *lock the door*? Why would she do that? Why do we have to get trapped literally everywhere we go today?"

Denver breathes out very slowly. "There's got to be a window or something, right?"

I nod. "Right! There's definitely a window." Except the large window at the front of the shop has those big iron bars on it. I don't actually remember seeing any other windows, which I would have found creepy if I hadn't been distracted by the dolls and human hair. The whole shop is dark and dusty.

"More creepy dolls," says Hudgie, nodding over to a giant bleacher display of them. There are steps and steps of dolls. Their faces are spiderwebbed with cracks, and most of them are missing an eye. Some of them are missing *both* eyes. "Aren't you scared of dolls, Truck Stop?"

"Just the creepy ones," I say. What I *don't* say is that they're all the creepy ones, in my opinion. But they are. Those scary glass eyeballs that pop open when you stand them up? No thanks.

Hudgie must remember what happened when we were in second grade. I was just a little kid. Our teacher, Ms. Munch, read us a book about a girl named Tina whose doll had a string, and the string got stuck, so the doll said "Help me" all the time. It wasn't even supposed to be scary. Tina was just sad about her broken doll. But it scared the actual crud out of me. It scared me so bad that I sat at the back of the classroom and hid my face in my arms and cried, as quietly as I could. But my teacher noticed, and she said, "Tacoma Jones! Are you okay? Is this too sad for you, dear? Don't worry! The doll will get fixed in the next chapter!" I appreciated the spoiler, but I was still scared to death.

Madison and Piper were in that class, too. They thought me being scared of dolls was the funniest thing they'd ever heard of. They started a club just to torment me. They called it the Creepy Doll Club, and they'd leave invitations on my desk all the time. Terrifying invitations, with pictures of dolls they'd drawn all over them.

To: Tacoma Jones

Join our Creepy Doll Club! We meet at recess and talk about all the times our dolls came awake in the middle of the night and tried to get us while we were sleeping. (It's a LOT of times.) See you at recess!

I stayed as far away from Madison and Piper as I could at recess, but it didn't matter. They would chant at me in the lunch line. "The dolls will get you, Tacoma Jones. They'll eat your ears and eat your bones!"

And now here I am, surrounded by them. The creepiest dolls on earth. Most of their clothes are torn, as if they'd been played with a long time ago. I step closer to the dolls, trying to feel braver than I really am. "Who would play with you?" I ask a doll with dirty fingerprints on her cheeks and no eyes. "You're *terrifying*."

"Little miiiiisssss," shrieks the doll, and I scream and back away, before realizing the voice was not coming from the doll but from somewhere behind the bleachers. I feel immediately relieved that I just used the restroom, or I would definitely have peed my pants in front of both Denver *and* Hudgie.

"Holy crap," says Hudgie. "That scared me to death."

Denver is clutching his chest and gasping for breath. "She's still in here! I thought for sure she'd locked us in and left."

"Little miiiiisssss."

My heart thumps loudly in my chest. "That's not her," I whisper. "Remember? Her voice was kind of rusty." *Like nails.* This voice is completely different. Familiar though, somehow.

"Little miss?"

The voice is closer.

"We need to hide," I whisper to Denver and Hudgie. Hudgie's eyes get wide.

We duck behind the bleacher display of dolls and crouch down low. Under dozens and dozens of horrible dolls.

The dolls will get you, Tacoma Jones. They'll eat your ears and eat your bones.

"Little girl, I *know* you are in here. I watched you come in and you didn't come out. Your friends, too."

Hudgie gulps.

Recognition chimes in my brain. "Hang on. You know who that sounds like?"

"Little miss? It's me, Denise. Or maybe you remember me as Raw Sugar? I just saved your butts, and now I'd like to know why you broke into Kyle Glenson's truck."

Denise. The raw sugar lady from the Brake Fast! Raw Sugar, the truck driver from the radio, is *Denise.*

CHAPTER 14

I scramble out from under the bleacher display. "Denise?" I crane my head to see over a table piled high with fingerless leather gloves next to the bleachers. Denise's head appears over the top of them.

"*There* you are." She hurries over to me. "I have about a thousand questions for you. Why'd you do it? What were you *thinking*? How are you planning to get home? And oh my *God*, why do you smell like that?" Denise covers her nose and mouth with her hands. "Start talking."

"Okay, it's a long story. But basically Kyle stole something from our truck stop and we snuck in to get it back."

"Did you get it?" Denise asks.

"Yes!"

"Good. But you coulda ended up in Boise, little miss. What you did is so dangerous! And illegal. You need to stay out of people's trucks or something truly terrible could happen to you."

"I know. And I won't do it again. And as for how we're going to get home . . ." I look back at Denver and Hudgie, who are getting out from under the bleacher display. Hudgie gives an awkward wave to Denise. "Well, I didn't know, but now I'm kinda hoping you could give us a ride?" I smile my nicest smile at Denise. She frowns.

"No way. I already lost an hour of driving because of you two! Also, you stink. I don't want that in my cab. You can use my phone to call your parents, though."

I sigh. "Okay, thanks."

Denise hands me her phone. "And just so you know, that Crocodile Kyle is awful. I just had the world's worst cup of coffee with the world's worst trucker, and you'd better be darn grateful. If I have to pay for coffee the next time I'm at the Brake Fast, I will be mightily offended."

"I am, and you won't," I say. "How did you know we were in the sleeper cab?"

"Well, you nearly ran smack into my truck back at the Grange. I recognized you from your parents' truck stop—you always make sure I've got some raw sugar hidden away in the kitchen and I never forget a kindness. It's rare enough out here on the road. I saw you get into Kyle's truck, which was strange, and then I saw that young man run in after you. He seemed mighty upset. Then Kyle got in and pulled out on the road, so I followed. I didn't know if you were being kidnapped on purpose or on accident. I wouldn't put anything past Kyle. Asked him who he was with, and he said just his nephew there, so I figured that was the boy I saw running, and either he was lying or you might've got yourself into something, and either way somebody needed to look out for you." Denise shrugs. "I did what I could to help. Wasn't expecting three of you, though."

"Well, thanks." I mean it. If it weren't for Denise, we really might have ended up in Boise without a way to get home. I look at the phone in my hand. "Actually . . . Do you mind if I make two quick calls?"

"If they're *very* quick." Denise taps on her wrist. "Time is money, literally. I gotta go."

"Thanks," I say.

The first thing I do is call the Brake Fast.

"Brake Fast Truck Stop," Mom answers.

"Mom!" It's so good to hear her voice. "We got a little sidetracked, but we'll be home in an hour or two. I hope that's okay!"

I hear a ton of noise in the background. Some kind of music, lots of laughing. My stomach does a little jump. I hope Dad's a part of all that. The music and the laughing.

"As long as you're safe, kiddo," Mom says. "I hope you're having a good time! I can tell you right now the band is. Hey, did you get those ingredients you need? You need to start thinking about dinner pretty soon here, if you're really going to make it."

My dinner.

"Don't worry about dinner. That's—that's what's taking us so long. We're figuring it out."

Denver looks at me skeptically.

"You be careful, and I'll see you soon."

"Hey, Mom?" I say.

"Yes, honey?"

"How is Dad doing?"

There's a silence. Denise taps her wrist again.

"He's still not feeling good, honey. But you know it's temporary. Just gotta stick with him through the hard times, and love him *all* the time."

My heart feels kind of heavy. I'm not there with him during *this* hard time. But I'm doing everything I can to bring his photo back home, and I sure do love him. All the time.

"I know. I'll be home soon, Mom," I say. I press the End button on the call.

"Figuring it out, huh?" Denver asks. He runs a hand through his hair.

"Tick tock," says Denise. "Time is money," she reminds me.

"Almost done," I say. "I'll make sure to throw in a muffin with your free coffee the next time you're at the Brake Fast. Just don't mention it to my parents."

Denise seems okay with this trade, so I quickly look up Hugh's number on the Grange's website. He puts his personal cell number right on the front page, because that's just how Hugh is. I call it.

"You've got Hugh," says Hugh.

"Hugh! It's Tacoma Jones, and I need your help."

Hudgie's face contorts. *Whyyyy*, he mouths.

"Whoa! Tacoma Jones twice in one day! Happy to help any way I can, of course. What's going on?"

"Well. Me and Denver and Hudgie are stuck in Ellensburg at some kind of Curiosities and Oddities shop. Right up the road from Olive's Juice-Up. Are you still in Cle Elum? You said you had to pick up some pumpkins there. I think Cle Elum is right next to Ellensburg, right?"

Hugh hoots. "It sure is! And I know exactly the place you're talking about. That place is wild! I'm on the road—haven't got my pumpkins yet, but if you don't mind stopping at the patch with me, then I'll come get you right now! I might be half an hour. Your parents are okay with this?"

I breathe the biggest sigh of relief. "That is perfect, Hugh. Yeah, my parents are really busy today, so they'd appreciate you getting me home." I mean, they are, and they would. So it's not a *total* lie. "Thank you so much. We'll meet you out front."

"But, uh, Tacoma?" Hugh's voice is a little less enthusiastic now.

"Yeah?"

"Hudgie needs to leave my pumpkins alone. You understand?"

I nod solemnly, even though Hugh can't see me. "I promise to take full responsibility for Hudgie. Thanks, Hugh."

I press End again and hand Denise her phone.

"See? That guy hates me," says Hudgie.

"That guy is about to rescue you from the Little Shop of Horrors, so practice gratitude," says Denver.

"Somehow, I kind of think we're going to be okay," I say to Denver. Then I remember the locked door and the barred window. "If we can figure out how to escape this place. Denise, you must have gotten in somehow, right?"

"Try the door," says a voice around the corner, like a jar of rusty nails. "That's the usual way. Maybe try a little reading comprehension this time."

I shiver.

"Let's go," I whisper to Denver, Hudgie, and Denise. "Thank you!" I call to the terrifying little woman who is somewhere in her shop, purple lips and all.

We make our way back to the door, which I now notice has a large *PUSH* sign above the handle. When I push on it, the door opens, and I breathe the second-biggest sigh of relief.

"Tacoma, were you . . . *pulling* on the door before?" Denver asks.

"Thank you for everything, Denise," I say quickly, and a little louder than I mean to. We step out into the sunlight. "I mean it. Without you, we'd be—"

"I know, you'd be working on a potato farm in Idaho trying to thumb a ride back this way," says Denise. "You're welcome." She winks at us and climbs up into the shiny green cab of her truck. We watch her start the ignition, shake out her hair, and pull out onto I-90.

"You clearly have very good luck," says Denver.

"I think lucky people don't get trapped in sleeper cabs, but I guess I've had a little." I sit down on a raised curb stop.

"Can you luck into a granola bar or something?" Hudgie sits down next to me. "Because I am so hungry."

"I mean, there's those jars of edible bugs inside, if you want," says Denver. "Or some hair."

Hudgie shudders, and I grin.

"What did you mean 'Don't worry about dinner'?" Denver asks. "Because I know you're dreaming big dreams today, but by the time we get back to the truck stop, I'm going to be ready to eat an *actual* truck. Shouldn't we just worry about getting back? I don't mind breakfast food. Except, uh, maybe not eggs. Maybe never eggs again," he says, sniffing.

I press my hands to my cheeks. "There's still plenty of time," I say. My dinner's got to happen. "Hugh's taking us to a pumpkin patch, and the bigger patches usually sell produce and stuff. I really think this is going to work out. A real dinner with gorgeous, locally grown produce." I imagine Guy Fieri giving me a high five. It's going to work out, because it has to. Even if it feels like there's definitely *not* enough time, and even though that feeling of panic is lying right there under the surface of me, waiting to rise like high tide over a beach. *It's not too much. I've got this, and I've got help. It's not too much. It's not too much.*

When Hugh's old blue pickup pulls into the parking lot, excitement practically bursts out of my face.

"Hugh!" I open the passenger door and climb to the middle of the bench seat, motioning for Denver and Hudgie to join me.

Denver hangs back. "Mm . . . This is a rooster-free ride, yes?"

Hugh's eyebrows shoot up to the center of his forehead in the most pitiful apologetic face I've ever seen. "No rooster, I promise. I'm really, really sorry about that, again. Tick Tick's at home. I keep the sound system on so he can listen to his favorite tunes."

Denver raises an eyebrow.

"Grateful Dead," Hugh explains. "The *American Beauty* album. It kind of mellows him out."

A sigh escapes from Denver and he climbs in next to me. Hudgie squishes in next to him and closes the door.

"Thank you so much for picking us up, Hugh," I say. "You would not believe the kind of day we're having."

Hugh sniffs and politely rolls down his window. The egg stink. "It must have been a weird one for the three of you to end up in Ellensburg with no ride back! Ellensburg is a wild, wild place." Hugh adjusts the volume of the radio. I don't recognize the music, but it's fast, and there's a fiddle. "You know what you can't find anywhere but Ellensburg? A blue agate." Hugh shakes his head, a big smile on his face. "Strangest, most beautiful rock you'll ever see. I found one once, when I was a kid. It looks like something that coulda dropped right off the moon. So wild."

"Cool," I say.

We pass a sign that says *Welcome to Cle Elum.*

"You know what Cle Elum's got?" Hugh asks.

"Pumpkins?" guesses Hudgie.

Hugh glances sharply at Hudgie, then back at the road.

"Well, yeah, pumpkins. But everywhere's got pumpkins this time of year. Cle Elum's famous for its meat vending machine. Some of the best steaks I've ever cooked up came out of that meat vending machine."

"A meat . . . vending machine?" Denver asks, a skeptical look on his face.

"You bet. Imagine being famous for a vending machine full of meat," says Hugh, laughing.

A flock of excited crows starts flapping around in my stomach. "Hey, Hugh, is there any chance we can stop at that meat vending machine on our way back?"

"Of course we can!" says Hugh. "Maybe a little rib eye will calm ol' Tick Tick down. Remind me after the pumpkin patch."

"Maybe you shouldn't be teaching him to like the taste of meat," Denver says, resting his head on the back of the seat. "I haven't taken a nap since I was, like, three years old. But I could use one now."

I grin. "I know what you mean." Except I don't feel tired at all. My body is exhausted, but my brain is working faster than it's worked in months. Seven people from the bus plus the three Joneses, that's ten. Hugh's coming, so eleven, and let's say seven extra for customers—that'll fill all the tables we have—so eighteen for dinner. Back at the truck stop we've got eggs, flour, sugar, salt, oats, milk—

"We're here!" Hugh says, pulling into a crowded parking lot under a rusty arched *Fraser Farm* sign. There's a giant orange-and-green field of pumpkins in front of us, big wooden bins of harvested corn and warty pastel pumpkins—the kind you put out for decoration, but you'd never eat—and an A-frame barn with a register on a table out front. There's an overwhelming expanse of twelve-foot-high corn behind us, across the little road, and way in the distance is Mount Rainier, covered in snow and capped with a flat whirl of clouds.

Click.

Click.

Denver lowers his camera. "This is such a Halloween *moment.* Farms aren't my usual vibe, but a pumpkin farm in October?"

"A pumpkin farm in October is *everybody's* vibe," says Hudgie, looking around appreciatively. If you like stomping pumpkins, this place probably feels like a candy store.

Denver grins at me.

Denver Cass doesn't do friends, and Hudgie Wilson is kind of my nemesis. But right here this afternoon, I almost feel like I have two friends where I didn't have any before. I try not to think about it too much, like it'll go away if I do. It's like when you wake up from a good dream. The harder you try to remember it, the faster it leaves you.

There are families wandering around with wheelbarrows full of pumpkins and arms full of bagged kettle corn. Kids are screaming—the good kind, not the bad kind—and grown-ups are drinking from steaming Styrofoam cups of coffee or hot cider, arranging their kids for pictures on hay bales and in front of the pumpkin patch, and clicking away.

A woman with a long brown braid over one shoulder: "Smile! Smile so big! Can I see your teeth? Smile big!"

A man in a flannel shirt with the sleeves rolled up to his elbows: "Let's get one of you jumping! Can you all jump on three? One . . . two . . . three! Cindy, you have to jump! Okay, let's try again . . ."

A woman with a heaping wheelbarrow: "No, no, honey, I know, but we already have our pumpkins. Our wheelbarrow's full! We can't fit any more . . . Okay, well, just a little one, then."

A woman with big glasses and a bun on top of her head: "Let Mommy blow on that cider first, buddy. It's so hot. Do you see the steam? That means it's hot. Let Mommy cool it down for you so you don't burn your tongue."

A little boy with blond hair and a very red face: "Please call them! Please!" He is clinging to an older girl's leg. "Tell them to come back!"

The older girl is looking at her phone. Her forehead is all wrinkled up like she's worried about something, and she seems totally oblivious to the little boy on her leg. He's crying now, real tears. "Please! I want my mom! I want my mom and my dad!"

The older girl shakes her head at something she sees on her phone. "This is not happening right now," she says. My face goes kind of hot. What is wrong with this girl? She doesn't seem to care at all that this little kid is upset.

"Please!" The little boy is sobbing now. "Please please please."

Hudgie is watching them, and his face looks kind of gray.

"Stooooop," whines the older girl. "I'm literally dealing with complete and total heartbreak right now. I need to talk to Mason and I can't do that with you yelling. You're being *so* selfish. Have a tantrum when you get *home*, okay?"

"Are you okay?" I ask Hudgie.

He shakes his head just slightly. "I don't like when—you know, kids are upset and nobody cares."

I remember the way Kyle talked to Hudgie back at the Grange. *You better not be crying about it.*

"Somebody should do something," murmurs Hudgie.

"Get off me! Don't you see that I'm *dealing* with something?" howls the girl.

The little boy startles and lets go of the girl's leg, sitting down hard on the dusty ground. His eyes squeeze shut again as fresh tears stream down his face.

Hudgie starts walking toward them. Denver, Hugh, and I follow, with Kyle's voice in my head.

You want to keep talkin'? Keep reminding me that you spilled your juice all over my truck? Because I'll take you home right this second. I already told your mother I don't have time to drag you all over the place.

The little boy is practically purple now, gulping air. Before we can reach him, he's on his feet and gone, running through the parking lot, then across the road. In a quick swish of ten-foot cornstalks, he disappears completely.

"Oh my God, are you *kidding* me right now? Like I don't have *enough* going on!" wails the girl, who is now finally looking up from her phone.

My heart is beating so fast. "He's in the cornfield!" I say. Denver points to a sign in front of the cornstalks. *Corn Maze, 12+ or must be accompanied by an adult. Prepared to be SCARED?*

That little boy is not 12+, and he's not accompanied by an adult. If I had to guess, I'd say he's *definitely* not prepared to be scared.

"You three wait here," says Hugh. "I'll go after him." He looks at the girl. "What's his name?"

The girl is furiously typing something on her phone. "Mm. What?" She glances at Hugh.

"What is his *name*?" Hugh looks angry. Angrier than he's ever looked at Hudgie.

"Oh. Um, it's Calvin."

Hugh takes off across the road, and he's swallowed by the corn. I can hear him yelling "Calvin!" as he disappears into the stalks.

The girl glances at her phone again with a frown, then tucks it into her back pocket and crosses her arms.

"Are you Calvin's sister?" I ask her.

"No. I'm babysitting."

"Okay, well, you're, like, *criminally* bad at babysitting," I say. "He was so upset, and you just ignored him."

"He's *always* upset. He always wants something—his mom and dad, or a snack, or just . . ." She gestures vaguely with both hands. "Something. What am I supposed to do about it? I'm dealing with a crisis, and he can't give me one minute to—"

"*He* is dealing with a crisis," Hudgie interrupts. "That little kid. When a little kid is screaming and crying? That means they're having a crisis."

As if on cue, a shriek echoes from somewhere inside the maze.

I look at Hudgie. Hudgie looks at me. *Prepared to be SCARED?* That poor little kid. We've got to do something.

"Hugh said to wait here for him," Denver says, reading my mind.

"I know he did," I say. "But we can't. He's a little kid, Denver. He's got to be scared to death. Remember how *bad* it feels to be scared to death? How many times have we been scared, just today alone?"

Denver chews on his bottom lip. "A few." He jams his hands into the pockets of his jeans and stretches backward, looking up at the sky. "Fine. Let's go."

But before we take a single step, Hudgie is already gone, running toward the corn maze with his fists balled up.

"Hey," I say to the babysitter. She doesn't look at me. She's looking at her phone again. "*Hey*," I yell.

This time she looks up. "*What?*"

"The man we're with—his name is Hugh. If he comes back here, tell him we went into the maze."

"Okay." She looks down at her phone again.

"Okay *what*?" I say, staring at her. I have the overwhelming urge to smack her phone right out of her hands and onto the ground.

"Okay, I'll tell him you're in the maze." She breathes in loudly through her nose and lets out a sigh that sounds more like a sad yodel. "I'm in the middle of, like, the second-worst breakup of my life. *Right* before Halloween. So I'm sorry if I'm not, like, Babysitter of the Year right now. We bought our costumes together! Am I supposed to just go as toothpaste? Without a toothbrush? That's not cute, it's just weird, and—"

Denver and I don't wait for her to finish. We take off after Hudgie.

"She's kind of the worst," I say.

"She's *definitely* the worst," Denver says. "Mason knows what's up. That's why he doesn't want to be her toothbrush."

We enter the maze the way Calvin, Hugh, and Hudgie did—not at the entrance, but through a wall of corn, bending the stalks to either side of us, disappearing completely in a rustle of leaves. It only takes a second to find the actual maze. We step into the narrow clearing and follow the path.

"Hugh," I yell. "Calvin! Hudgie!"

The corn is so high it blocks out almost everything else, including the sun, and all I can see is cornstalks and a straight blue stretch of sky.

"Do you think Calvin realizes he's in a maze?" Denver asks. "Do you think he's following it, or do you think he's just running through the walls?"

"I'm not sure." The corn isn't moving, other than a shush-y collective rustle in the wind every once in a while, but it feels like it's closing in anyway.

No. This wasn't supposed to happen. None of it. Anxiety stirs around inside me like chunks of celery in a noodle soup, rising slowly to the top. We've been derailed too many times today. I just need to get my dad's picture back on the wall. I need to get back in time to make dinner—and soon enough that Mom and Dad don't worry. Because the last thing Dad needs on a bad day is to worry about me. Dad's hard days happen when they happen, and there's no telling when they're going to be. But me going missing is one of the things that'll make him anxious if he isn't already there, and it'll make his hard day so much worse. It's happened before, a few years ago, when I was ten.

We went to the Saturday farmer's market in Issaquah. Mom sent us. She said we could both use some fresh air, and that she'd take care of the Brake Fast.

The farmer's market is like a miniature fair, with booths and buckets full of peonies and lilacs; trays and trays of broccoli, lettuce, and radishes in more colors than just red; and food trucks all circled up, with lines of people waiting at the windows. Dad pointed out the Italian sausage food truck. It's the best one, and kind of famous this side of Seattle—they take a big piece of Italian bread, hollow it out a little, and stuff it full of sausage and peppers and the best sauce I've ever had in my whole life. Guy Fieri even had them on his show once.

"Italian sausage for lunch?" Dad asked.

My mouth watered right as soon as he said it, like Pavlov's dogs. "Definitely," I said.

We got in line, and I saw a booth just past the truck circle that sold honey. There were little golden jars stacked high on the counter, and big see-through pitchers with dozens of honey sticks all fanned out in them. There were shelves of beeswax soaps with a honeycomb pattern on them, and beeswax candles just like the ones at the Grange, shaped like snails and rabbits.

But the best thing about the honey booth was the giant glass-framed beehive, crawling with dark, fuzzy bees.

"Look at that!" I said to Dad.

"Very cool," Dad said back, but he wasn't looking at the bees. He was looking at the guy who'd just picked up his Italian sausage from the window. The bread was so big he had to hold it with both hands.

"It's real bees," I said.

"Yeah," said Dad, but he still wasn't looking at the bees.

"Be right back," I said.

I wove around lines at the other food trucks and made my way to the bees. They were kind of cute, but kind of scary, too, crawling all over each other, all buzzing at the same time so the whole hive seemed like it was groaning and humming.

"Pretty neat, aren't they?" asked the girl behind the counter. She had long blond hair with streaks of pink and green underneath. Her T-shirt was tie-dyed and said PLEASE SEES MY BEES.

"I like your shirt," I said.

The girl looked down at her shirt like she'd forgotten what she was wearing. "Thanks! Me and my moms wear these shirts at every farmer's market."

Her and her moms. For the first time ever, I'd met another kid who worked with her parents.

"How old are you?" I asked.

"Twelve! How about you?"

"I'm ten, and I run a truck stop with my mom and dad in North Bend!"

The girl reached out for a low five.

I slapped her hand lightly, feeling a little heat creep up my neck. I didn't high- or low-five people very often.

"That's awesome. Seriously, I love working with my moms. Bees are my life. Like, they're literally the reason everything exists. Food, oxygen. Think about it."

I nodded. "Ycah, bees are . . . great."

I wished I could sound more passionate about bees in that moment, but I didn't know how to. The girl didn't seem to notice or mind.

"Do you like running a truck stop?" she asked.

"I love it," I said. "I get to cook for truckers all day long and hear all kinds of amazing stories about the rest of America. They drive all over. I want to do that, too, someday."

The girl raised her eyebrows. "Be a trucker?"

"Drive all over. In my own food truck."

Food truck.

As soon as I said it, I realized I'd been gone too long. I should have gone back to the line already. I turned around and scanned the food truck lines. Dad wasn't in the Italian sausage line. Dad wasn't in *any* of the lines.

"You okay?" the girl asked.

"Yeah, I just—" Everything felt like it was moving a little slower except for my pulse. That was racing. I stepped a little shakily out from in front of the honey booth and looked down rows of produce and flowers. "My dad." My voice sounded strange and far away. "I can't find my dad."

"It's not a very big market." The girl brushed her long hair off of one shoulder. "I'm sure he won't get lost." She grinned at me.

It kind of felt like I'd been in a delicate bubble of *same* for a minute, where I was talking to another kid who spent her weekends running her family business with her parents just like I did.

"Dad?" I called out.

"Seriously, he's got to be around here somewhere! Just chill," said the girl.

Pop. There went the bubble. We weren't the same anymore. She didn't know about how certain things could set off a panic attack in a parent. She didn't know how a panic attack could completely derail that parent, making them beyond anxious and scared and not able to drive home. She didn't know how that panic and anxiety could empty itself right into depression, like a creek feeding into a river, or a river feeding into an ocean.

That was exactly what happened. When I found Dad, he was sitting on a folding chair outside a coffee booth, his elbows on his lap, his face in his shaking hands. He was trying to take deep breaths, and there was a lot of concerned mumbling behind him from the people running the coffee booth.

"Dad?" I said.

He looked up at me, and my heart sank. His face was gray-white and all creased, like a piece of paper somebody had crushed up in their hand. "Kiddo," he said. "There you are." His voice sounded crushed up, too.

"I'm sorry. I'm really sorry. I just went over to look at the bees for a second, but I stayed gone too long. Dad? I'm sorry."

"Your mom is coming," Dad said, really slow, like he had to dig his words out from behind that wall.

"She's coming here?" I asked. "Are we—are we going home? Aren't you hungry?"

Dad didn't say anything else.

Sometimes the depression is like a river, and sometimes it's an ocean. I could tell then that this was going to be one of the ocean times.

"Why don't you just sit here with your dad, honey," said one of the coffee ladies. "Seems he's having a hard time. Your mom's coming. You just wait here."

I sat down on the ground next to Dad, and I wanted to be home so bad. Home, where nobody could see what was happening. I wiped away tears of embarrassment with the heel of my hand. I hated feeling like that, but we were out in the open, in front of a lot of people. Dad wasn't upstairs in his room above the Brake Fast, he was sitting in front of the coffee booth trying to take deep breaths, his face all crinkled up, while all kinds of people walked by. Some pretended not to look, and some couldn't look away.

When Mom showed up, her eyes were red like she'd been crying. She held on to Dad and we all got in her car, and nobody said anything. The Brake Fast stayed closed all afternoon, which it'd never done before.

That was the last time I'd gone missing on my dad, until today, when I can't seem to *stop* going missing.

Denver and I turn a corner in the maze.

"*Aaaaaahhh!*" I scream. There is a scarecrow, ten feet tall and wearing a black fishing hat and long black trench coat, lurking in a cutout in one of the corn walls. His stick arms are poised to reach for us with their skeletal twig fingers. *Prepared to be SCARED?*

"No," says Denver, squeezing his eyes shut. "This is not for me."

"It's not for me, either," I say. "And it's definitely not for little kids. Poor Calvin."

Denver cups his hands around his mouth. "Calvin! Caaalll-viiinn!"

We keep walking. There are voices in the distance, but it's hard to tell where they're coming from or if they're even any of the people we're looking for. Somewhere to the right of us, deep in the corn, a crow *kraw kraaaaw*s loudly.

"I don't tell people the actual scariest thing that's happened to me," Denver says. "Because it's not so much a scary story as an awful story, you know?"

I know exactly. I nod.

We turn a corner.

Denver takes a deep breath. "Last Christmas, me and my mom and the band were all staying at a hotel in Las Vegas. One of those *really* swanky hotels. We never have a *traditional* Christmas—no tree or stockings or anything like that. We're on the road. But

Mom must have been feeling festive, and she asked Daryl, the old drummer, to grab a taxi, get to a store, and bring back a box of Christmas cookies. Daryl said, 'Oh, I don't know, Nan, I'm not feeling too good, and anyways I don't know what's what in this city. If you want dessert, why don't you order room service?' But Ma's mind was made up. 'No, it's gotta be Christmas cookies.' So I said I'd go. I was bored anyway. And I thought maybe I could get some pictures of the Strip. Ma wouldn't let me go alone. She was like, 'You're barely a teenager, I'm not sending you out into Las Vegas by yourself on Christmas Eve.' So Daryl said fine, he'd come with me. We get a cab and sit in the back. Daryl tells me he misses his wife and daughter. He tells me he's got a daughter with Down syndrome and she's the best thing that ever happened to him. He tells me he's got a horse back home, a rehabilitated horse. That horse was a racehorse until he got hurt, and he was going to be put down, but Daryl rescued him and now he's living in this mansion in New Jersey, the luckiest horse on the planet. He tells me he's been writing a book all about his time on the road, and he's going to dedicate it to his wife and daughter. That he does all this for them, because this is the only thing he knows how to do. He tells me—" Denver's voice breaks.

We both stop walking.

"He tells me the band members are his brothers and my mom is like a sister, and he's been so lucky to see me grow up. He tells me to listen to my mom, and that I'm gonna do big things someday. He tells me he wants me to have his camera—this Nikon I take everywhere. And his face is really red at this point, and he's sweating. And something about the way he's talking is just freaking me out. He kind of sits forward and rests his forehead against the back of the driver's seat. I say to the driver, 'Hey, can you please get us to a hospital? This man needs to get to a hospital.' So we go to a hospital, and they meet us outside with a stretcher, and they take Daryl away. And my mom shows up with all the guys a little while later, and I just cry my freaking brains out in that waiting room, hugging my mom. And after a while, it was past midnight. It was Christmas. And a doctor came down and told us Daryl died."

I look at Denver and tears are streaming down his face. He doesn't try to stop them or wipe them away. He just lets them fall on his bear sweater.

"I'm so sorry," I say. "That's horrible."

My toes feel numb from how horrible it is, but I don't ever know what to do when somebody is crying in front of me. Touch his arm? Say *It's okay*? Of course not. It isn't okay.

"Yeah." Denver clears his throat. "So we got a new drummer. And I take Daryl's camera with me everywhere. But I think about his wife and daughter and horse all the time."

"What was it? I mean, how did he die?" I ask.

"Nobody would tell me. I guess it was a heart attack or something, but it seemed like he knew it was happening. He was talking so strangely in the cab. The things he was saying before he died."

Denver takes a deep breath, and then he looks at me. "So. That was my scariest, most awful thing. I've never told anybody that before."

Two crows chase each other overhead.

My heart feels like it's racing, because my scariest, most awful thing is still in my head where no one else can see it, making my breath fast and shallow until I have to count the things I can see, the things I can hear, and the things I can feel.

One. Denver. Two. The corn. Three. Hay on the path. Four. Those crows. Five. The blue streak of sky.

"Mine was at that tunnel. Where we found Hudgie."

"Wait, today?" Denver asks.

"No, last year," I say.

Denver nods, like *Go ahead.*

"Me and my dad were walking through it. My dad . . . he has depression and severe anxiety. Sometimes it gets pretty bad. Most of the time he's super creative and fun, but sometimes he spends a few days or weeks in bed. We were walking through the tunnel last year, and my dad was feeling bad. I knew as soon as we got there. But I was . . . I don't know. Selfish, I guess. I didn't *want* him to be depressed. He didn't want to go in, but I talked him into it. I told him that we'd be fine, it'd be fun. So we went in. When you're walking in this dark tunnel talking to somebody, and they're talking back to you, it feels okay. Like earlier today. I mean, it's creepy, but it's okay. When you're walking with somebody who is shutting down, it doesn't feel okay at all. I started to panic. I kept saying things to him to try to get him to talk—to hear my own voice in the dark, maybe—and eventually he couldn't go on any farther. He kind of collapsed somewhere near the middle, the darkest part, and he was just shaking and crying. I've never seen my dad like that before. He has bad days and weeks, and he goes to bed, and me and my mom kind of take care of each other and him. It's okay. But it wasn't okay in the tunnel. We weren't home. We were alone, and I couldn't help. I couldn't do anything for him."

I realize I'm talking fast. I want to get it all out of me. The whole story. I've only thrown up a few times in my life, but when I do, Mom is there to rub my back and tell me, "You gotta let it out, baby. You'll feel better when it's all out of you." This feels like that. Letting out what needs to come out. I'll feel better once it's all out of me.

"So I kind of sat down next to him and hugged him and told him it was going to be okay. But he said he wasn't sure. He said he loved me very much, but he just didn't feel like anything was going to be okay ever again." I swallow a sob that's trying to get out of my throat. I hear my voice getting louder and faster, but I don't care. "He said he couldn't do this anymore, and I didn't know what he meant. I kept asking, 'The tunnel? Is that what you mean? You just can't keep going in the tunnel?' But I kind of knew that wasn't what he meant. And we just stayed like that, crying, him all hunched over and me hugging him. He kept saying 'I can't do this anymore.' I knew I needed to get help, but I also knew I couldn't leave him there, alone in the dark. There's no reception in the tunnel, so I couldn't call my mom. We just stayed like that." My voice breaks. The despair of being that helpless in the dark with my dad isn't a memory. The dark is a memory, but the despair is *now* and *all* the time. Whenever the memory works its way back into my brain like a cephalopod, strong, cold, and slimy.

"Tacoma," Denver says quietly. "I'm so sorry."

"We stayed like that for a really long time. Maybe a couple of hours, I don't know. I kept hoping somebody would come down the tunnel. Somebody who knew what to do, you know? Somebody who could handle it. Finally I kind of got my dad to stand up, and we started walking back. Really slow. He leaned on me the whole way. By the time we got to the entrance, it was dark out. I used Dad's phone to call Mom, and she picked us up. Dad decided he needed to check into a hospital that night. He was in the hospital for about a week, and then he did a day program a week after that. When he came home for good—for days and nights—he was doing a lot better. But I hate thinking about what happened. Like, it keeps creeping into my head, and it's like I'm still in that tunnel, in the dark, more scared than I've ever been, and I hate it so much."

I can't talk anymore because I'm crying too hard.

Denver tucks me under his arm and gives me a long squeeze.

I guess that's a thing you can do when somebody's crying in front of you.

After a minute, my breathing has calmed down and he lets go.

"You okay?" he asks.

"Yeah," I say. I do feel okay, actually. Sad, but okay. It kind of feels good to get it out of me.

"Honestly, same," says Denver, and for a moment, things really do feel kind of okay.

There's a loud cracking, rustling sound up ahead of us. "Truck Stop?" calls a snuffly, very familiar voice.

CHAPTER 16

"Hudgie?" I run ahead and hear Denver's quick footsteps behind me.

"We need help!" Hudgie yells.

When we find them, maybe fifteen feet ahead, they're sitting in a maze cutout underneath a horrible scarecrow with jagged metal teeth and tuna-can eyes.

"The kid has kind of, um, a problem," says Hudgie.

The scene in front of me is really hard to process. First of all, there's the scarecrow. But then there's Hudgie, with his arm around Calvin's shoulders. Sort of like he's being kind and supportive to a scared kid, which I've never seen Hudgie do before. There's also the kid, who has obviously been crying. His breathing is shuddery and shallow, like mine was a minute ago. His face is dirty, with clean lines running down his cheeks where the tears washed them. He wipes some tears and dirt away from his eyes with the heels of his hands. There is a very rusty-looking nail sticking out the bottom of his sneaker.

"Ohhh my God," Denver says, in a voice that sounds on the verge of absolute panic. "I can't . . . No. I . . . That's a nail. It's sticking out of his foot. Oh my God, there is a rusty nail sticking out of that kid's *foot*! I really cannot do blood!"

"Shhh," Hudgie and I hiss at the same time.

Calvin starts sobbing again, his whole small body shaking.

I kneel down in front of him. "You're okay, buddy. I've stepped on half a dozen rusty nails in my life. We just need to get you out of the maze, okay?"

"You've stepped on half a dozen rusty *nails*?" Denver practically shrieks, still looking away. "How? When? *Why?*"

"Yes! Stop yelling, you're freaking this kid out. I don't know, playing in the lot behind the truck stop. When they tore down the shower buildings, they left some nails and stuff. The truckers thought it was funny. They would say, 'Thanks for keeping that one out of my tire, Tacoma!'"

"And you didn't *die*?" Denver is holding his head with both hands like he's worried it's going to fall off.

"Am I going to *die*?" wails Calvin.

"No!" Hudgie and I both yell.

"Why would there be a rusty nail just chilling in a corn maze, anyway? What kind of horror farm *is* this? 'Come for the corn, stay for the tetanus!' Is this how the great state of Oregon celebrates Halloween? With fields of torture?"

"Washington," says Hudgie.

I turn to Denver and make my eyes as big as I can. "It's not a big deal. Nobody's getting tetanus. Sometimes old nails and bolts and pieces of equipment come up when they turn the ground. It's a totally normal thing. This is not a 'field of torture.' *Please* stop freaking this little kid out. Okay?"

Denver takes a shaky breath. "I refuse to accept that it's a totally normal thing. But you're going to be okay, kid. My friend Tacoma is going to get you out of here, and you're going to be fine."

My mouth drops open in shock. "Denver Cass! We *are* friends! You said you didn't do friends, but then you just called me your friend!"

Denver waves dismissively. "Probably because I'm in shock. I'm saying all kinds of strange things. Maybe I don't do blood *more* than I don't do friends, okay?"

"Nope. You said it, and it counts."

"Hey, guys?" Hudgie says. "Can you help me stand him up?"

I bend over and sling one of Calvin's arms over my neck, helping him to his one good foot.

"Kids?" Hugh shouts from somewhere nearby. "Aren't you supposed to be waiting *outside* the maze?"

"Hudgie found Calvin, but he's hurt," I yell back. "Can you get to us?"

"Yeah, on my way."

There is rustling from somewhere in the maze.

"But seriously. Do you know if you've had a tetanus shot?" Denver asks Calvin.

"*Denver*," I say.

"I don't know." Calvin sniffs. "I *hate* shots."

"Don't worry about it," I tell him. "Hey, did your babysitter drive you here?" I ask, suddenly realizing that the girl is going to be no help at all, even if we manage to get Calvin out of the maze.

"Shelly doesn't drive. My mom and dad dropped us off. They're going to come back to pick us up. But *please* don't leave me with her. All she cares about is her boyfriend."

Hudgie stands up and ruffles Calvin's hair.

"We'll get you out of here, and then we'll stay with you until your parents get back. Okay?" says Hudgie. "Trust me, I know what it's like when somebody's supposed to take care of you, but they treat you bad."

"Can you guys talk a little louder?" Hugh calls through the corn. "So I can find you?" He sounds closer.

"Hudgie, about that," I say. "Your uncle Kyle shouldn't ever talk to you the way he does. You're a . . . pretty good kid, and you don't deserve the stuff he says."

Hudgie shrugs. "I steal stuff from his truck."

"Clearly you should find a hobby," says Denver. "Stealing is *not* it. But even so, he's a grown man, and you're a kid. Nobody should talk to a kid like that. Not ever."

Hudgie nods thoughtfully.

The wall of corn in front of us splits open and Hugh steps through. "Buddy! They found you! Are you doing okay?"

Calvin sniffs.

"Hudgie found him," says Denver.

Hugh raises his eyebrows in surprise and looks at Hudgie. "You did! Well done, Hudgie."

Hudgie almost-smiles down at his shoes. "Yeah. Thanks."

Calvin makes a small whimpering sound, and Hugh's attention snaps to his foot. "What happened?"

"He stepped on a nail," I say. "We need to help him out of here."

Hugh holds his arms out to Calvin. "I'm happy to carry you back to the parking lot, little guy."

"No!" Calvin looks up at Hugh, his face red with fury. "I can do it myself."

"I'm sure you can, but you've got a hurt paw there, and I—"

"Let's hop," I say to Calvin. "Ready?"

Calvin wipes a hand across his eyes, clearly trying to be brave. "Ready."

I help him stand up and wrap his arm around my neck. I have to kind of hunch down, because he's a lot shorter than I am. He lifts his nail-foot knee and hops on the other foot, trying it out.

"Why do you all smell so bad?" Calvin asks, looking back and forth between me and Hudgie.

"Rotten egg," I say.

Calvin nods as though that's all the explanation he needs.

I take a slow step, with Calvin's arm around my neck, and wait for him to hop forward. He does. We take another step that way, and another.

"We've got it," I say. "How do we get out?"

Hugh's face falls a little bit. I look at Denver, and he's picking a piece of corn silk off of his bear sweater.

"I think that's the point of the corn maze, Tacoma," he says. "It's supposed to be hard to get out."

"Only if you're following the rules," I remind him. "If you're not, and we aren't, then you can bust through corn walls until you're out."

Hugh looks up at the sky. "I wish I could see the mountain from inside the maze. The corn's too high. If I could see the mountain, I could get us out."

Denver opens his eyes. "If we're all really quiet for a minute, maybe we can hear the road. We'll want to go that way."

We're all silent. I feel Calvin shift a little and remember that his foot probably really hurts.

"You're being a super-brave kid, just so you know," I whisper. There's not much I can do for Calvin. He still has a crappy babysitter and a nail sticking out of his foot. But I can help him out of this maze, and I can be nice to him. That's something, I guess.

In the distance, there is a *zhoooo* sound from a passing car. Then another.

"There we go," says Denver, pulling himself off the ground. "We need to go this way."

We follow Denver through corn walls and open sections of maze, holding our hands up as shields so corn leaves don't thwap us in the eyeballs.

We finally break through the last wall of the maze and we're on the road across from the pumpkin patch.

"Mom!" yells Calvin. "Dad! That's my mom and dad!"

There is a couple standing with Shelly-the-terrible-babysitter, looking incredibly worried. As soon as they look up and see Calvin, lines disappear from their foreheads, and they run across the parking lot toward us. We meet them at the entrance.

"Oh my God, baby." Calvin's mom grabs Calvin by the shoulders and pulls him into a giant hug.

"Ow, careful," says Calvin, pulling back a little. "There's a nail in my foot."

His mother recoils. "A *nail*?"

"Oh, buddy," says Calvin's dad, inspecting Calvin's foot. "We need to bring you to the doctor. Let's get you in the car, okay?"

Calvin shoots me a worried look.

"Don't worry," I say. "Remember? I've stepped on half a dozen of these things. You're going to be totally fine. And you'll have a cool story to tell afterward."

Calvin tries to smile. He looks at Hudgie. "Thanks for finding me."

Hudgie smiles back, but it's a sad-looking smile. "You're welcome, buddy." He looks at Calvin's mom and dad and shoves his hands in his pockets. "You should know that Shelly was the reason he ran into the corn. She was ignoring him. He was really upset, asking for you guys, and she didn't care." Hudgie glances at me, Denver, and Hugh. "She treated him really badly. We all saw it."

"Neglect," says Denver. "It was textbook neglect."

Calvin's parents' mouths are kind of hanging open.

"Shelly?" the dad calls in a scary-calm voice.

"Yeah?" Shelly asks nervously, approaching from behind them.

"Get in the car," says Calvin's mom, her voice even calmer and somehow even scarier. "After we get Calvin to the hospital, we're going to take you home, and we're going to talk to your parents about what you did here today."

"What *I* did?" Shelly's face crinkles up in disbelief. "He ran away from me! I didn't do anything!"

"That's the problem," says Calvin's dad. "You didn't *do* anything."

Shelly's mouth drops open. "I was *about* to. But just so you know, I am having a *very* hard time." She wiggles her phone so we can all see it. "I'm going through a *breakup*."

"Calvin is going through a *nail* in his foot!" I screech.

Shelly's lip curls at me. "Ew," she mutters, and stalks off toward the cars.

"Thank you all. What you did for Calvin today— I'm just so glad you found him," says Calvin's mom.

"We're in the market for a new babysitter," says Calvin's dad. "If any of you are interested."

"In fact, let us pay you for today." Calvin's mom pulls out her wallet and hands me three twenty-dollar bills.

"Whoa!" says Hudgie. "Thanks!"

"That's really not necessary!" I protest. "He needed help, so we just . . . helped."

"It is, actually." Calvin's mom glares in the direction that Shelly disappeared. "I don't even want to think about what could have happened to my son if you hadn't been here."

A man in a flannel shirt and sunglasses walks over to our group. "Is this the little boy? Did everything turn out okay?"

"This is the little boy, but I don't know how well things turned out," says the mom. "He has a rusty nail sticking out of his foot! We're taking him to the emergency room now. You really should check your corn maze. Children run around in there, for Pete's sake."

The man in the flannel shirt visibly pales. "Oh my." He looks down at Calvin's foot and gets even paler. He seems to think quickly and come to a decision. "Oh *my*. I . . . How would you folks like to help yourselves to some of our products? Free of charge, of course."

"We're not going to sue you, if that's what you're worried about," says Calvin's dad. "But you really ought to check the maze for nails before you have kids walking through it."

"Anything you want," says the man. "We've got all kinds of stuff! Cornmeal, rice, peppers, onions, corn on the cob, squash, potatoes, really, help yourselves."

"We're fine," says Calvin's dad.

"Actually, could *we* take you up on it?" I scan the bins of produce across the parking lot. *My dinner. It's really going to happen.*

"Oh, sick!" says Hudgie. "I forgot about your dinner. And I'm *starving*." Hudgie glances at me, embarrassed. "I mean, if it's okay, I'd like to come for dinner."

Denver grins at me. "You really are going to make that dinner, Tacoma Jones."

A flutter of excitement runs through me. I really am going to make that dinner. "Of course you can come," I say to Hudgie. *Because we're friends*, I say just in my head.

"For the heroes of the day? Of course," says the man in the flannel shirt. "Take a few bags and fill 'em up. I'll tell my employees not to hassle you."

"Thank you, all four of you," Calvin's mom says to us.

But I'm barely paying attention. In my head, I'm scanning through pages of my cookbooks. Squash casserole from *Old Virginia's Southern Kitchen*. Au gratin potatoes from *Best Spud Recipes in Idaho*. Cornbread from *Lone Starters and Apps: The Joy of Texas Entertaining.*

"Let's go shopping," I say to Denver and Hudgie.

This is going to be the best night the Brake Fast has ever had. It's going to be one of the best nights *any* of us has ever had.

We load our sacks of food and about thirty pumpkins—the ones Hugh came here for—into the back of Hugh's truck.

"What a day," Hugh says, sliding into the seat of his truck. "What an unbelievable day."

"You don't know the half of it," says Hudgie.

I shoot him a look, because I don't need Hugh to find out about us stowing away in Kyle's truck. Hugh is cool, but he's not keeps-crimes-a-secret-from-your-parents cool.

"We heading back to the Brake Fast?" Hugh asks me.

"Actually, can we go to that meat vending machine you were telling us about?"

"Oh, right. Forgot in all the excitement. Sure thing, Tacoma. It's over at Owens Meats, not far from here. That's right—you're making a real dinner tonight!"

"I sure am," I say.

Hugh whistles. "An unbelievable day. Your mom and dad gonna help?"

"No," I say. I get kind of a weird feeling in my stomach, like nervousness and pride all mixed up together. "I'm making this one. By myself."

"No you're not," says Denver. "I'm going to help."

"Me too," says Hudgie.

I sit back in the bench seat, not minding that my elbows are smooshed between Denver and Hudgie. Just enjoying the company. Enjoying being someplace comfortable like Hugh's truck after a whole day of uncomfortable places.

We drive in silence for a couple of minutes. The sun is starting to sag in the sky, turning everything a glow-y kind of orange.

Hugh pulls into the parking lot of a little redbrick building with a big *Owens Meats* mural painted on the side.

"Why don't you take that money from Calvin's folks and put it toward your dinner?" Hugh suggests. "Here, I'll throw in a few dollars, too. Dinner sounds awful good right about now."

"Are you sure?" I look back and forth from Denver to Hudgie.

"Yeah. It's yours. So long as that counts toward my dinner bill," says Hudgie.

"Thanks, guys." I flick through the money from Mom in my pocket, the twenties from Calvin's parents, and the wad of cash Hugh hands me. I elbow Hudgie to open the door and jump out, so I can get out of the truck.

The vending machine is full of smoked sausages, pepperoni, cheese, smoked fish. B9 is andouille sausage. My *Cooking Cajun and Creole in Louisiana* cookbook has a great-looking jambalaya recipe. I slide a twenty-dollar bill into the slot, then another and another, until all the money is gone. I make my selection, and hand-wrapped packages of refrigerated sausage thud to the bottom of the vending machine. I gather them up and get back in the truck, this time on the passenger side instead of in the middle.

"Ready?" Hugh asks.

"Ready," Denver, Hudgie, and I say at the same time.

"I'm looking forward to your dinner, Tacoma Jones. I'm pretty hungry," says Hugh.

My stomach growls as if on cue.

"Tell me about it," says Denver. "We haven't eaten since breakfast."

"You could've had those edible bugs," I remind him.

He shudders.

"Here," I say, reaching into one of the bags from the pumpkin patch. I pull out a small bag of kettle corn and hand it to Denver.

"Tacoma Jones, saving lives again," says Denver, his mouth already full of popcorn.

The drive home is long. Hudgie nods off at some point, his head kind of plopped onto one shoulder. The sun sets farther behind the mountains, and the gray road in front of us winds through the pass like a snake, calm and graceful. I wonder if this is what Denver sees all the time. The road, taking him from one music venue to another, state to state to state. I'd never get bored of driving like this.

By the time the truck stop appears in the windshield, the night is fully dark. The Brake Fast windows glow warm and bright, and it kind of reminds me of driving around with Dad this last December, looking at all the Christmas lights and the lit-up trees in neighborhood windows.

"How about that one?" Dad nudged me and pointed to a three-story house, covered from top to bottom in strings of white lights. There was a giant green wreath—real-looking—hanging on the front door, and a single candle in every window.

"Too fancy," I said to Dad. "Like it's in a movie or something."

Dad grunted his agreement. "Way too fancy."

We kept driving.

"What about that one?" I pointed ahead of us to a house with big air-filled Christmas mascots all over the yard. Rudolph, Frosty, the Grinch, and Snoopy, all bloated like Macy's balloons and shivering in the wind.

"Too inflatable," said Dad.

"Way too inflatable," I agreed.

We drove past some more houses—some without lights, some lit up with Seahawks blue and green lights, some with those giant old-fashioned red, green, orange, and blue bulbs just along the roof line.

Then I saw the house. "Dad," I said, patting his arm. "That's the one, right? It's perfect." It was a one-story house with a big window in the front. You could see the tree inside, lit up with a million tiny gold-white lights. There were more lights hung in the big window, strung along the roof, draped over the rhododendron by the front door. But the best part was the family of deer on the small front lawn. They were made out of some kind of branches woven through with more lights.

"You found it," said Dad. "The perfect Creepy Christmas Cocoa house."

He pulled the car over and parked right in front of the house. The lit-up deer were so close I could have touched them if my window were open. Dad turned off his headlights and handed me one of the cups of cocoa in the double cupholder between our seats. I turned up the volume on the radio. A jingly commercial voice sang, "WARM 106.9 . . . Your home for Seattle's holiday favorites."

"Remember last year's Creepy Christmas Cocoa house?" I grinned at Dad.

He squeezed his eyes shut and rubbed his forehead, laughing tiredly. "Oh no . . . Don't remind me. That was the first time we actually got *called* creepy."

I leaned my head back on the headrest and laughed, the cocoa warming my hands.

"The lady looked so mad, stomping up to the car and knocking on the window." I shook my head and took a sip of cocoa. It was so hot it nearly burned my tongue, but I didn't care.

"'Exactly *what* are you doing parked all creepy in front of my house?'" Dad's impression was so good, I almost snorted cocoa out my nose.

"Oh man, remember when you told her how we do this every year—'Ma'am, every year we look for the best house to have cocoa in front of'—and that she won? And she was like—"

"'I've *won*? Well. That changes things. What have I won?'" Dad was laughing so hard, tears streamed down his face and he wiped them away with the back of his hand.

"And I said—"

"'Us! Drinking cocoa in front of your house, ma'am! Would you like some?'" Dad's impression of me was perfect, too. We both howled, laughing until our stomachs cramped up.

Except it's not Christmas, it's almost Halloween. And the warm light coming from the Brake Fast isn't because of trees or candles or lit-up deer. It's because of all the people inside it, animatedly moving around near the windows like those dancing mannequins in that scene from *Home Alone*. Mom and everybody from the tour bus, plus whichever of our regular customers have come by tonight and any passing travelers who happened to stop. Maybe even Dad. It's a really cozy scene when you look at it like this.

The perfect house.

When I'm not at school, I'm at the truck stop, so I never really get that feeling of *Oh man, it's good to be home.* How can you miss somewhere you never leave? But I have it now.

I nudge Hudgie awake. He shifts beside me and lets out a grunt.

I grin at Denver.

"Let's get cooking," I say.

The door jangles when we step inside. Our arms are full of sacks of groceries from the pumpkin patch. It's warm and bustling, and there are jackets and sweatshirts strewn around.

Nick Jersey is perched on a step that leads to our apartment upstairs, playing his guitar while another guy from the band nods along and plucks a few strings of his bass.

"Holy cow, I thought I'd never see you again." Mom hurries over and kisses me on the cheek, but she's smiling. Her face is pink and warm, and she smells like vanilla.

"The trick," she told me last year, "is vanilla extract." We were sitting on hard plastic chairs in the waiting room at the hospital. Our visit with Dad was scheduled for noon, but Mom liked to go early, just in case they'd give us extra time with him.

"I've known a lot of women to spend all kinds of money on perfumes that smell exactly like vanilla extract. I just use vanilla extract! We've got it in the kitchen. Dab a little bit on your wrists and behind your ears, and you'll always smell sweet. Plus, it really covers up the smell of bacon grease."

When the nurse brought us in to see Dad—at twelve o'clock sharp, never any earlier, though it didn't stop Mom from hoping—he got up out of his chair and rushed over to hug us both. He wasn't wearing a hospital gown or anything like that—he wore a gray T-shirt and sweatpants, and his hair was wet from a shower. He looked healthy. He looked better than he had before he went there. He breathed in deep when he hugged Mom.

"You smell really good," he told her.

She winked at me. "Vanilla extract."

Now, in the entrance of the Brake Fast, I'm the one who breathes her in. "Sorry we were gone so long," I say. "We had kind of an adventure."

"You were about due an adventure, kiddo. Let's get you warmed up and you can start on your dinner! We've got a lot of hungry people here." She looks at the bags we're holding. "*Wow.* You really did go shopping."

"Sure did," I say.

Mom looks at me proudly, and I *feel* proud. Wait till she sees the photo I got back for us. For Dad. Wait till she tries my dinner. Wait till she sees what I can do.

I look around the dining room. Dad isn't there.

Mom notices me looking for him. "He's resting in his room, baby. He'll be okay." She leans toward me and whispers in my ear. "But I've gotta tell you, you smell a little funky. I don't think even vanilla is going to help with this one. You might want to change your shirt, or something."

Right, the egg stink. I leave my sack on the stairs and run up to my room. I change into a fresh sweatshirt. I roll up the egg-stink shirt and shove it way down in the hamper. I try not to look at Dad's closed bedroom door on my way back downstairs.

I collect the sack of squash and peppers and round up Denver, Hudgie, and Hugh. "You guys can put your bags in the kitchen. Denver and Hudgie, if you really want to help, wash up and grab aprons off the hook by the stove."

"You got it," says Hugh. He clears his throat. "But, ah, Denver, I'd love an introduction, if you have a minute first."

Denver looks puzzled for a second, and then realization pulls at the corners of his mouth. "Oh, right! You want to meet my mom."

Hugh grins. "I do! John Denver's tour bus driver, I mean, *man*. Man! An absolute legend."

"Who's a legend?" Denver's mom calls from the other end of the dining room. The restroom door closes behind her. "Denver Cass, I can't wait to hear what you've been up to all day. If you are a legend now, that's got to be a great story! You get some good pictures?"

Denver gestures to her with his camera in his hand. "Sure did. Mom, this is Hugh. He's a big John Denver fan."

Denver's mom sits down at a table and pats the tabletop. She swishes her long hair over her shoulder. "Well, Hugh, come take a seat. I never get tired of talking about that man. I've got some stories I bet you'd really like to hear, and my ungrateful son over there doesn't let me tell *him* anymore!" Hugh makes kind of a weird face—smiling and dopey—sets down the bag of corn, and practically floats over to the table before landing in the seat across from Denver's mom.

"Ready to cook?" I ask Denver and Hudgie.

"Yup," says Hudgie. "You mind if I call my mom first? I don't want her to think I'm still in Ellensburg. And maybe she could come have dinner with us?"

"Definitely," I say.

"I'm ready," says Denver, but he's looking suspiciously at his mom and Hugh.

CHAPTER 18

The first thing you need to do in the kitchen is clean. The counters, your hands—you just need everything to be clean. The second thing you do is practice *mise en place.* Get out your kitchen equipment and the ingredients. You don't want to realize you don't have what you need halfway through cooking. That'll throw the timing all off.

Mise en place. My heart starts beating fast in my chest, because I really can put everything in its place tonight.

"Denver, can I get that picture out of your bag?" I ask.

Denver unzips his camera case and pulls out my dad's photo. He hands it to me. "Somehow, Tacoma, you're pulling it off," he says. "You got the photo back, and you're making dinner for everybody. Just like you said."

I hug the photo to my chest. "Not *somehow.* I did it with a lot of help. From my friends." The word *friends* feels really good to say, especially when you actually *have* friends, which I think I do for maybe the first time in my life.

I duck through the dining room, winding around chairs that've been moved around and instrument cases that are leaned against tables and wide open on the floor. I hang the photo back on the wall, exactly where it used to be. Nobody even notices me, but the whole room feels different. Better.

Back in the kitchen, I search my collection of cookbooks for the ones I need on my shelf by the pantry. Kitchen space is at a premium, but storing my cookbooks here was a deal I made with my parents when I reminded them my allowance isn't minimum wage, and I work a *lot*.

"What're we making, Chef?" Denver asks. I know he's kind of joking, but a tiny jolt of electricity zips down my spine when he calls me *chef*.

I pull down *Lone Starters and Apps: The Joy of Texas Entertaining* and open to the cornbread recipe. I lay it on the counter. "Cornbread from Texas," I say to Denver. I pull down a second cookbook. *Old Virginia's Southern Kitchen.* "Squash casserole from Virginia." *Best Spud Recipes in Idaho.* "Au gratin potatoes from Idaho." *Cooking Cajun and Creole in Louisiana.* "Jambalaya from Louisiana." *Bay State Tastes Great: Massachusetts Desserts and Treats.* "Pumpkin pie from Massachusetts. Hudgie, can you ask Hugh if we can have a couple of the pumpkins from his truck?"

"Uh, yeah. He's gonna make me promise not to stomp them, though. Don't people usually just use a can for pumpkin pie?" Hudgie asks. "My mom does."

"Hudgie Wilson, *nothing* is from a can tonight," I say.

He shrugs and leaves the kitchen to find Hugh. I set Denver up with a cutting board, a knife, and some green peppers and onions. After I show him how to chop them, he takes over like a pro.

"With bus school, you have to be *really* good at following directions." He shrugs modestly.

I start slicing potatoes into thin circles. I measure out the cornmeal and dump it into bowls with flour, baking powder, and salt. When you're making something like cake or cornbread, you have to mix the dry ingredients first, then you can add the wet ingredients. The eggs, the vegetable oil, the buttermilk. That way you know it's well mixed. I cut the andouille sausage into thick coins and sauté them in a heavy pan. I transfer them to a plate when they're browned, and sauté the chopped onion, the peppers, some celery, and garlic after that. I'm surprised by how easy it all seems. I guess you learn a few techniques, even while cooking nothing but breakfast every day. Sausage is sausage, after all.

Hudgie comes back, holding two round pumpkins like they're twin babies. "All yours," he says.

"Thanks! Rinse them off, and then you have to wash your hands again."

Hudgie makes a face. "I washed my hands like two minutes ago!"

"But then you went outside and picked up pumpkins and touched doorknobs. You've gotta wash them again."

Hudgie sighs and brings the pumpkins over to the sink. "Cooking is a *lot* of work."

Denver cracks a smile, blinking away tears from the onions.

I measure out the dry rice and dump it on top of the vegetables, then cover it all with chicken stock and crushed tomatoes. I shake some spices on top—paprika, salt, garlic powder, black pepper, white pepper, onion powder, oregano, cayenne, thyme. I give it all a good stir and cover it with a lid.

"Hudgie, I'm going to work on the potatoes. I need you to make the pie crusts, okay? I'll tell you how to do it."

Hudgie bites his lip. "Pie crust. You're gonna trust me to make your pie crust?"

I realize with a jolt that I *do* trust Hudgie to make my pie crust. Because Hudgie Wilson isn't nearly as terrible or untrustworthy as I thought he was. He's my friend. And he's going to help me make a pie.

"Yeah, I am. Because you rescued a hurt kid today, Hudgie. *And* you stood up for him. That was brave. Half of cooking is just being brave."

Hudgie shrugs. "If I was brave, I'd have told off my uncle Kyle a long time ago. I guess I always felt like if I don't have Uncle Kyle, who do I have, you know? I don't have a dad. My friends are jerks."

"We disagree," says Denver. "Those guys with you in the tunnel were jerks. *We*"—he gestures to me and to himself—"are amazing."

My face practically cracks in half from smiling.

Hudgie grins and rubs a hand over his hair. "Thanks, Denver."

Denver sighs and returns to the cutting board. "I kind of miss 'Funeral Barbie.'"

I pull a few sticks of butter out of the fridge. "Hudgie, you have to wash your hands again before you start on the crust."

"Why?" Hudgie holds up his still-damp hands. "I just washed my hands a whole second time!"

"Yeah, but you touched your hair after you washed them."

Hudgie sighs and walks back to the sink.

Once Hudgie's hands are clean, the three of us are like a hurricane in the kitchen. I'm shouting ingredients and instructions to Denver and Hudgie, while I cut squash for the casserole, make the cheese sauce for the potatoes, and roast and mash giant pumpkin wedges. I catch Mom peeking in to check on us a few times, but she must be okay with what she sees, because she doesn't say anything. Hudgie takes direction really well. I knew he would. He needs some help fluting the edges of the crusts (I mean, in both of our defense, it's kind of hard to just tell somebody how to flute a crust), but that's all. I pour in the pumpkin pie filling, and then we let out one big breath. The ovens are full, the jambalaya is simmering on the stove, and our job is mostly done, for now.

"Let's put more coffee on," I say.

"It's what, seven o'clock at night?" Denver checks the clock over his shoulder. "Seven fifteen! Who drinks coffee this late at night?"

"First of all, this is a truck stop we're running. Truckers come in and order coffee till closing. Lots of them drive through the night. And second, we're not going to serve pumpkin pie without coffee to go with it," I say. "C'mon." I hold my hands out like *What are you thinking?*

Denver laughs. "*C'mon,*" he parrots. "Are we some kind of weirdos who serve pumpkin pie without coffee? What would the Pilgrims think?"

Hudgie cracks up.

I laugh with them both, and right there in the warm kitchen full of new, wonderful smells—*dinner* smells—I think I'm probably happier than I've ever been in my whole life. I'm with my *friends*, fresh from our wild day, and we're home at the Brake Fast cooking dinner—*dinner*—and my dad is out there in the dining room, I can hear him, and . . .

Dad.

I get a feeling in my stomach, like helium, like a balloon that's so full it could burst any second.

He's down in the dining room, where I was hoping he'd be. I can show him that I got his picture back. Maybe that'll make him feel a little bit better. And we'll all eat together. My *dinner*.

The coffee grinder makes its low, comforting growl.

"I'm so hungry, I think my stomach has started eating itself," says Hudgie. "Can I just grab a bagel or something to tide me over? Maybe an apple? Everything smells so good, it's torture!"

"Don't even think about filling up on bagels and apples!" I say. "Dinner will be ready in another twenty minutes. Why don't you two take drink orders in the dining room? We've got all the fountain drinks you see on the machine, plus coffee, milk, and iced tea, sweetened and unsweetened." I take two order pads and pens from the shelf next to the walk-in fridge. "Take these." I hand one to Hudgie and the other to Denver.

"Thanks." Denver gestures toward me with his pen. "Just so you know, I'm putting this all on my résumé someday. 'Sous-chef, waiter at the Brake Fast.' I'm putting you down as a reference."

"You'd better!" I grin. "Don't forget Official Photographer!"

Denver grins and follows Hudgie out of the kitchen, ready to take drink orders. I lean against the counter and take a deep breath in. This late in October, it's just starting to feel like the beginning of the cold season, so the warmth of the kitchen is extra nice. Everything really is working out today.

Then Dad appears in the doorway to the kitchen. My heart does a squeeze in my chest. His face is still gray, and his hair is mussed up like he's been sleeping. He has purple circles under his eyes, and deep creases at the corners of his mouth.

"Dad," I say. "You aren't going to believe what I got." Excitement rises in me like the hot-air balloons Dad took me to see in Winthrop when I was a little kid.

Dad's face somehow gets even more tired-looking. "Later, okay, kiddo?" He kind of shuffles through the kitchen. Slowly, like he's sleepwalking. He's holding the water glass from his nightstand. He fills it at the sink.

"Your picture! It's hanging on the wall again," I say. "The one that went missing! The one of you with Bruce Springsteen!"

Dad turns off the water. He looks thoughtful and a little more interested. "Oh wow. All right. That's great. Thanks, kiddo."

He starts shuffling back toward the kitchen door.

"*And* I'm making dinner for everybody. Just like we planned. Only, I'm making jambalaya and potatoes, and—"

Dad winces and holds up his hand in front of his face, like he's trying to ward off a headache. "*Okay*, kiddo. Thank you."

He leaves the kitchen, and I feel like all the air was let out of me.

I know that it's just bodies and brains, and I can't fix anything when Dad's feeling like this. But as I follow Dad into the bright dining room where everybody else is so *happy*, the sharp difference in Dad feels like somebody's pressing their finger into a bruise on my heart.

Denver and Hudgie are writing down drink orders and Hugh is listening in a happy daze to Denver's mom. The band is spread out, softly playing instruments and laughing together, and Nick Jersey is telling Mom a story, talking with his hands. It's warm and cheerful in here, and it smells like dinner—my dinner, a dinner that would probably make Guy Fieri say, "Holy moly, stromboli." I got the picture back, and everything should feel right. But Dad is headed to the stairs, barely registering any of this. Panic rises in me again.

Don't go.

Don't go!

If Dad isn't here, my dinner won't be right. Nothing will be right.

"Tacoma, honey, how's dinner coming?" Mom asks. Her words are normal, but her voice is low and slow, like she can see the anxiety in me.

"Um, it's, uh—" I can't get the words out, and I can't seem to get deep enough breaths in. Dad disappears upstairs.

I hear one of my timers go off in the kitchen, but I can barely move. The linoleum might as well be quicksand.

"Dad isn't feeling good today, honey," Mom says quietly. "It's okay. That happens, and he'll be all right. He's handling it and things are under control. Now, how are *you* feeling?"

I shake my head to clear it. "Good!" I'm not. "I'm good. I got dinner going in the kitchen, and I got Dad's Bruce Springsteen picture back, so everything is really great, actually. It's great." I try to slow my breathing down. Deep breath. Let it out.

"Hold on. *How* did you get his picture back?" Mom narrows her eyes. "Didn't you tell me that *Kyle* stole his picture?"

My stomach clenches up. This isn't how tonight is supposed to go. "It's kind of a long story. My timer's going off and we've got to get dinner served to all these people, so let's talk about it another day."

Mom stands up. "No, I think we're gonna talk about it today. Right now. I'm happy to help you get your dinner plated." She jabs a finger toward the kitchen door. "Kitchen. Now."

I take the long route to the kitchen, all the way around the counter, feeling like I've got a sack of Hugh's pumpkins weighing me down. We slip our hands into oven mitts and pull out the pies. I turn down the burner on the stove and give the jambalaya one good stir.

"Did you break into Kyle's house?" Mom asks me. She spins around and crosses her arms, still wearing the oven mitts.

I could say no, because I didn't *technically* break into Kyle's house, but that still kind of feels like a lie, and I'm not going to lie to my mom. Not tonight. But I *do* think I can sidestep the question a little bit. "It was in his truck."

"How'd you get in his truck?"

"Hudgie helped. He's Kyle's nephew."

Mom purses her lips and nods.

"Does Kyle know?"

I'm actually not sure if Kyle knows, now that I think about it. I shrug. "He will eventually, I'm sure."

"Well, I like the intention behind what you did. I don't like the sneaking around, but I do like that you tried to do something nice. Something that you're *never* going to do again, right?"

I give a short nod.

"It's your night, honey. You've been wanting to cook dinner since you were old enough to *say* dinner, and judging by the way this whole place smells, you've done an incredible job." Mom adjusts the pies on the cooling racks and slips off her oven mitts. "Now, your dad's got depression, and today's one of those days. Do you know why that's hard on your heart?"

I rest my hand over my bruised-feeling heart.

"It's because you love him. And it's because you've got the same thing in you that your dad and I have in *us*. You take *care* of people. That's what this truck stop's about. That's what cooking's about. It's just taking care of people."

It's just taking care of people.

Last year . . . That was Dad's worst time. His bad two weeks. The weeks he needed to be in the hospital because it all felt like too much for him to handle here at home. The words he said to me in the tunnel come back and buzz in my ears. *I can't do this anymore. I'm so sorry. I can't do this anymore.*

Anxiety and fear start to chew me up right there in the kitchen, starting with my fingers and toes, then my wrists and ankles, arms and legs. It feels like a bad kind of tingling, like I can't get enough air for my body to work the way it's supposed to.

When this happens, I know what it's called. I know what I'm supposed to do.

Do your grounding exercises, Tacoma. Dad's therapist gave us all tools to deal with the anxiety and panic. *Name your fears. Ground yourself in what is real, and what is right there in front of you. Five things you see. Five things you hear. Five things you feel.*

Name your fears.

I didn't take care of my dad.

Name your fears.

I didn't take care of him when I wanted to go into the tunnel. I didn't stop even when I knew he wasn't okay. I pretended I didn't know he was panicking. I pretended I didn't see him struggling. I cared more about pretending everything was fine than I did about my dad.

Name your fears.

My dad wanted to stop being alive last year.

Name your fears.

My dad will stop wanting to be alive again.

Name your—

My dad will stop living. He won't make it to the hospital next time. He will make that choice and then we won't have him anymore.

My breath is shallow and fast, and everything feels numb—my face, my limbs. My vision is narrow, and kind of gray around the edges. *This is a panic attack. You've named your fears. Now do the rest.*

Five things I see.

The two pies cooling on their racks, the color of leaves, pottery, rust. The low blue-orange flame underneath the jambalaya pot. My sneakers, crusted in dirt from this long day—the bike rides, the tunnel, the Grange, the corn maze—the stainless steel coffee maker, dripping dark coffee, steady and steaming, into the coffeepot. My mom kneeling next to me, pulling me down against her, her hands warm and her face worried.

"Sweet girl, you've got to do your deep breathing. You're all right. Everything's all right."

I shake my head. "Dad isn't all right."

I hear Mom take a sharp breath. She lets it out slow. "Dad's not all right today. But he's all right *enough*. You know what that means?"

I shake my head again.

"It means he's pretty low-feeling. But he's doing what he needs to do to get through it. He's got people who love him *so* much." Mom lays her cheek on top of my head. "That's you and me. We love him so much. And he's got a job he loves. He loves to cook, honey, just like you do. He's got medicine that helps a lot. And he's got the best therapist in Seattle. And you know what? If things get too hard for him, he even has a great hospital he can go to for a couple of weeks, just like he did last year. So he's all right *enough*."

I don't know why, but hot tears start to pour out of my eyes. I mean, *pour*. They're running down my cheeks, plopping onto my sweatshirt, making it really hard to see anything but blurry colors. "I didn't take care of him last year. I didn't do anything to take care of him, and he had to go to the hospital."

Mom lifts her face off of my head and looks at me, shocked. "Tacoma Jones, what on earth are you talking about?"

"Last year. Dad and I went on that bike ride, and we were going to walk through the Snoqualmie Tunnel, but he started to feel bad, and I ignored it, and by the time we were in the middle—"

"Oh, no, honey." Mom pulls away a little and holds me by both of my shoulders, looking me square in the face. "No. That had nothing to do with you. Okay? Your dad has a mental illness. Sometimes that *really* stinks. It stinks for us, and most of all it stinks for him. It is never, ever because of something you did or didn't do. Do you understand?"

I nod. "Yeah, and I know that. In my brain I know that. But it's like you said, I'd like to be able to take care of him and sometimes I don't know how."

"You did take care of him, sweet girl. You took care of him by *being* there with him. That's all he needed at that moment, and it's what you did. You being there was enough. You remember what I always, always say?"

She pulls me into a big hug, and I close my eyes, letting more tears fall, this time onto Mom's back.

"Stick with him through the hard times." I sniff. "And love him *all* the time."

"That is exactly right," Mom says into my hair. "And that's what you did."

I squeeze her tighter.

Another egg timer goes off, and I pull away, wiping my face on my apron.

"That's the squash casserole, the au gratin potatoes, and the cornbread," I say. "I should get them out." The jambalaya is already done, and the pies should be finished cooling by the time we're done serving dinner. I pull myself off the floor and hold out a hand for Mom. She takes it and pulls herself up.

"What can I do to help, Chef?" she asks. That tiny jolt of electricity zips up my spine again. *Chef.*

"I'm going to start plating foods, and you can deliver them."

Mom winks at me. "After we wash our hands, of course."

We wash our hands in the sink and I pull down a stack of plates and bowls and start ladling jambalaya into the bowls.

Hudgie rushes into the kitchen, with Denver right behind him. "Okay, how do I bring out the drinks? Do I balance a tray on my head, or . . ."

Mom hands Hudgie a tray. "You can just hold the tray in your hands, honey. That's traditionally how we do it here."

Denver grins at my mom and takes a second tray. "Thanks for clearing that up." He fills cups at the soda fountain.

I scoop bright yellow squash casserole onto plates, and white-brown portions of potatoes next to them. I cut the steaming cornbread into wedges and carefully lift them from the big cast-iron skillet.

Mom takes two plates—the jambalaya bowls settled near the edge—into the dining room, and everyone erupts into cheering.

"This is all Tacoma!" I hear Mom say. "Save the standing ovation for the real chef!"

My face is glowing from the steaming food I'm plating, and from my mom sounding so proud of me, and from the lightness in my body that wasn't there just a few minutes ago. Dad's upstairs, and he's all right *enough*, and what I can do is stick with him and love him. *You took care of him by being there with him.* I feel like I've been carrying around boulders in my backpack all year, and someone just dumped them out for me. Inexplicably, I still feel like crying. But good tears, I think. *Relief* tears.

Mom comes back into the kitchen and plants a big kiss on top of my head. "First of all, you're amazing. Second of all, I'm starving, and handing this food off is kind of like torture. Let's get it all out there so you and I can sit down and eat it!"

I beam at her. "Thanks, Mom."

We finish serving all the food, except for the pies.

There is talking and laughter in the dining room while everyone eats. When most of the plates are clear, Hugh stands up and starts clapping, really slow, like in a movie. Mom is next to me in our booth. She joins him. Then Denver, then Hudgie, and then everyone. The whole dining room stands up, and they're clapping, and I feel like my face is going to burst into flames, that's how much heat is in my cheeks, but I don't mind. I stand and do a quick little bow.

"Tacoma Jones," Mom says. "This is phenomenal. I mean, it's incredible. I want to eat this every day."

My heart does a hop inside my chest. "*Every* day? I mean . . . Can I do this every night?"

Mom shakes her head.

"No way. You have school. And you're twelve. And this is the Brake Fast. You're not going to be in charge of dinner every night."

I sigh. "Yeah, I guess so."

"But," says Mom, "I think you can make dinner on the weekends. We'll call it a special. And only when you want to. When it really is special."

"Thank you!" I hug her as tight as I can, glowing from the inside out. "You won't be sorry! Dinner every weekend? And I can make all kinds of different stuff?"

"You clearly can," says Mom, waving her hand over her plate. "I'm so impressed, Tacoma. Your dad will be impressed, too. We'll make him a plate for later, okay?"

I feel glow-y inside, sitting there with Mom, eating a dinner I made with my *friends*. Real friends. Friends who took care of me today. Friends I took care of, too. I left my anxiety on the kitchen floor, and I wish Dad were down here eating with us, but things are pretty good. *All right enough.*

The little bell above the front door jingles, and Mom and I turn to see who it is.

Standing there, with his big hat tipped over his mad-as-a-wet-cat face, is Crocodile Kyle Glenson, flanked by Hudgie's mom and two serious-looking police officers.

"Well, I'd be suspicious if *something* didn't go wrong once in a while," says Mom quietly, just to me. "But I kinda thought one Crocodile Kyle visit was enough for today."

My stomach suddenly feels full of cement, like it'll drop out of my butt and through the floor. *Police.* Kyle knows what we did, and he called the *police.* I look at Denver. He's watching Kyle and the police, his eyes huge, frozen with his fork halfway to his mouth.

"Mom?" Hudgie looks from his mom to Kyle.

Hudgie's mom looks like she's been crying. "It's going to be all right, Hudgie. No matter what happens, it's going to be all right."

No matter what happens? What did Kyle tell Hudgie's mom? The worry and sadness in Hudgie's face stabs right through me. His mom joins him at his table, with tears rolling down her face. Kyle and the police stay standing.

"Well, that's nice," says Kyle, through gritted teeth. "I see you got your picture back." He points to the picture on the wall, then sneers at me. Nobody else seems to see it because they're all looking toward the picture. Sneaky mean. Kyle nudges one of the police officers.

"There she is, Officer Louie! There's the little thief I told you about."

"It's Officer Lewis," says the police officer, clearly annoyed. "And please don't touch me, sir."

Kyle narrows his eyes at me and gestures toward the little table by the door. "Can I buy you officers a coffee? I got a long story to tell, and I'd like to do it with a nice cup of coffee in front of me."

"This isn't a movie, sir," says Officer Lewis. "Stop with the drama and get on with it."

Kyle looks a little ruffled. He plops down in a seat at the table, crossing his arms in front of him. The two police officers stay by the door. "I'll take a coffee just for myself, if you don't mind," Kyle calls to Mom with a sickly-sweet voice. "If you ain't too busy, that is."

Mom looks at me, calm and concerned. I nod at her. *It's okay. I'm okay. This'll be okay.* "Yeah, sure, Kyle." She disappears into the kitchen.

I take a slow breath in, hearing my heart bang against the inside of my chest. *Five things.* Kyle's gold tooth, flashing, mean, under the lights. Those two police officers, looking around like they don't want to be here. The sign on the door—facing me, it says *CLOSED*. It says *OPEN* the other way around, so customers know we're open. I wish we'd flipped it early tonight. Dad's picture on the wall. Half-empty sweetener and creamer bowls on all the tables. I let out that same breath, slow and quiet.

"See, I was gonna go to Boise today," Kyle says, "when I got a little chilly. It's getting cold out there. You know. Almost November."

"Sir," warns Officer Lewis.

Kyle waves him off. "I'm getting to it. So I went back into my sleeper cab, and what do you know? Somebody'd been in there. Somebody'd stolen from me."

"No they hadn't," I say. There's a scared tremble in my voice, so I ball my hands into fists and force it out. "Because it isn't called *stealing* if they're just getting it back."

Kyle pulls his lip back over his teeth, almost like he's growling. "Somebody'd been in my sleeper cab. That's where I sleep. That's unsettling, ain't it? You'd find it unsettling if somebody'd gone through *your* bedroom. Right, Officer Louie?"

"Sir, please just get to the point," says Officer Lewis.

"Well, then I got to thinkin'. If somebody'd been inside my cab, they could've been inside the back of my truck, too."

Oh no. All the indignation in me rushes out. The back of Kyle's truck. The stolen SnoBalls. I'm about to be in a whole world of trouble.

Mom appears again, this time with a mug and the coffeepot. She sets the mug down in front of Kyle and fills it up. She goes back to our booth, never taking her eyes off Kyle.

"Sure enough, I go into the back of my truck, and I see that I'm missing about half of my load! *Half* of my *load*."

I suck in air through my teeth. Half his load? How many crates of SnoBalls had Hudgie and those kids stolen?

"We didn't have anything to do with that," says Denver.

No, Denver. Don't get involved. The last thing I want is for anybody else to get in trouble for what I did.

"And I'm supposed to believe that?" Kyle snarls.

"You should believe him," says Hudgie. "Because he didn't take the SnoBalls."

Every head in the diner, mine and Denver's included, whips around to look at Hudgie.

"Now how could you know that, unless you took them yourself?" sneers Kyle.

"Oh, Hudgie," Hudgie's mom quietly sobs. "We're going to figure this out."

Hudgie puts a hand over his mom's hand, but he doesn't look away from Kyle.

Brave, Hudgie, I think.

"Now hold on," I say. "You need to hear what Hudgie was really up to today. He saved a lost little kid. And stood up for him. He took care of him when the kid was scared and alone. He's kind of a hero."

When I woke up this morning, I sure wouldn't have imagined defending Hudgie Wilson to a whole truck stop full of people.

Hudgie's mom looks at Hudgie in surprise. Hudgie sits up a little straighter.

"You wait just a minute," says Kyle, unsettled by the approving murmurs in the room. Hudgie sinks down again.

"No, *you* wait a minute," says Denver. All eyes turn to him. "Seeing that kid treated so badly probably felt super familiar to Hudgie because he's been treated horribly by his uncle Kyle." Denver glares at Kyle. "Maybe *abusively* is a better word for it."

"Excuse me?" asks Hudgie's mom, real quiet. Except she's not looking at Denver. She's looking back and forth between Kyle and Hudgie.

"That's bull. They're trying to get out of trouble here, by uh, by deflecting. Well, that ain't gonna work. Your no-good son took those SnoBalls and he's going to pay for it!" He jabs a finger toward Hudgie's mom.

"Thirty seconds ago you said Tacoma did it," Denver reminds everybody. "It doesn't seem like you have any evidence of anything at all."

"Hold on," says Officer Lewis. "What exactly do you mean by *abusively*?"

Before Denver can answer, Hudgie leans forward. "Denver's right. Uncle Kyle's never treated me like you're supposed to treat kids. He yells at me all the time. He says I'm worthless. He says *awful* things to me. I thought I deserved it because I'm such a screwup. He *told* me I deserved it. But I don't. Nobody deserves that."

The entire dining room is silent now, looking from Hudgie to Kyle. Kyle's mouth opens and closes. Hudgie doesn't seem to know what to say now that he's stopped talking, but he suddenly leans forward again.

"Oh, and just today, Uncle Kyle abandoned me at a truck stop in Ellensburg so he could go on a date."

"Excuse me?" asks Hudgie's mom again.

Kyle recoils. "That is not what—"

"Ellensburg?" Mom looks at me and raises an eyebrow. I realize there's a *lot* I'm going to have to tell her.

"We're getting offtrack!" shouts Kyle. "I don't care about the darned SnoBalls!"

"You sure seemed to care about them a moment ago when you were accusing my son," says Hudgie's mom. She isn't crying anymore. She looks *mad*. She wraps an arm around Hudgie, who looks some combination of happy and embarrassed.

"Never mind that," says Kyle, trying to regain control of the situation. "*That* one broke into my truck," he points a finger at me. "She stole my personal property. *That* is against the law, and *that* is why we're here."

His *personal property*? No, Crocodile Kyle chose the wrong night to come to the Brake Fast.

I get up. I walk calmly over to Kyle's table and sit down opposite him. Both police officers look suddenly more interested in the scene in front of them. I guess the twelve-year-old girl facing down the big, angry trucker is a *little* like a movie. My heart is hammering so hard against my chest I wouldn't be surprised if Kyle could hear it, but I don't let it show on my face. I will not be bullied tonight. "You know what, Kyle?" I say. "Let's go ahead and tell everyone here about this picture. Let's tell them about *all* the pictures."

The other police officer—the one who isn't Officer Lewis—nods at me to keep going, so I do.

"Kyle Glenson stole it from here a long time ago. Kept it on the wall by his bed like a prize. With about fifty other photos."

"You don't need to—" Kyle starts.

"I think I *do* need to," I say. "When I got our picture back, I saw all kinds of photos that don't look like they belong to Kyle. Pictures of people with their families, pictures of horses. Even a fishing-boat picture of Brandi Carlile. The kinds of pictures you see on diner walls. Which is exactly where my dad's picture was hanging before Kyle stole it."

"A fishing-boat picture of Brandi Carlile? The singer?" asks Officer Lewis. "Like the one that was stolen off the wall from that café in Maple Valley?" He looks Kyle up and down and frowns. "*That's* a coincidence, isn't it."

One or two of the band members are still eating their food. Most are watching the scene in front of the door.

Kyle stands up again. "Well now, that ain't the whole story," he says, pointing a finger at me, and then at Officer Lewis.

"Get your finger out of my face, sir," says Officer Lewis.

"You go around stealing from diners?" asks the other police officer. "And you keep those items in your cab like crime trophies?" He shakes his head, pulls a notepad out of his back pocket, and writes something in it with a tiny pencil. "*That's* unsettling."

"Not like crime trophies," sputters Kyle. "Like *souvenirs*. Harmless souvenirs from where I've been! Now just you wait a minute, Officer Murphy. Don't be writing anything down yet, because this girl broke into my truck, stole that picture, and left some kinda stink bomb, or . . . I don't know what. But my truck smells *awful*."

Mom raises an eyebrow at me. She remembers the way I smelled when I came home.

"Oh, actually," interrupts Hudgie, "the egg was me. I had it in my pocket on that ride-along with you. Before you called me worthless, yelled in my face, and abandoned me."

"Now listen here, you little—" hisses Kyle.

Hudgie's mom stands up before he can finish. "No, *you* listen, Kyle. You're not going to talk to my son that way anymore."

Kyle looks shocked. He's probably not used to people standing up to him, and tonight it seems like everybody is.

I clear my throat before he can respond to his sister. "You did just admit to stealing, right? From all kinds of establishments like ours?" I raise my eyebrows at the police officers. I hope they wrote down what he said.

Officer Lewis shakes his head in disgust.

Kyle turns toward me, burning red, clearly more comfortable confronting a kid again instead of a grown woman. "Now, I don't know what you're trying to do here, miss, but breaking and entering is a felony here in this state of Washington, and that's exactly what you—"

"Nope," says Officer Murphy, looking at his little notebook over the top of his glasses. "You're thinking of burglary. Burglary is a felony. But it doesn't sound like this young girl's the one who burgled."

Officer Lewis scratches his neck. "It's up to you if you wanna press charges, Mr. Glenson. But I gotta tell you, it doesn't look so good for you. I don't like what I heard that young girl say. Or that young boy. Or your nephew, either. Sounds like you did more than burgle. You created a public disturbance, you abused and neglected a minor, and I'm sure there are a few more . . ."

"Stop." The color's drained from Kyle's face. He doesn't even look mad anymore. Just defeated. He sits down across from me again and kind of slumps in his seat. "I . . . won't press charges."

Relief rolls over me like a wave.

Officer Murphy tucks his notebook back into his pocket. "Swell," he says sarcastically. He nods at us. "Sorry for the disruption, everybody."

"Probably not as sorry as Kyle," I say.

The dining room erupts with laughter. Even Officer Murphy and Officer Lewis are smiling.

"We'll let you all get back to your pancakes," says Officer Murphy, turning to leave.

"No pancakes tonight, Officer. Can I interest you in some jambalaya?" Mom asks, smiling proudly. "My daughter, Tacoma, made it herself."

The way she says it—proud and puffed-up like that—makes me feel kind of warm all over, and like I might cry, especially after everything that just happened.

"Jambalaya at the Brake Fast? Huh. How about that," says Officer Lewis.

The police nod their goodbyes and escort Kyle into the parking lot. All he leaves behind at the Brake Fast are a dirty look my way and a cup of still-steaming coffee on the table.

I get up from where I'm sitting and look around the dining room. Most of the diners have finished their food. "Who wants pumpkin pie?" I ask.

Some of them cheer. Some of them yell things out, like "Yes, please!"

Hudgie's mom is holding Hudgie's hands in hers, and there are tear streaks down both of their cheeks.

"I'm sorry," she's saying. "I didn't know."

After we eat the pies and drink the coffee, Nick Jersey stands up on his chair. I'm pretty sure if it were anybody else, except maybe Bruce Springsteen, Mom would ask him to get down.

"We've got a little treat for everybody," Nick says. "A little something we've been working on today."

I look at Mom across the booth to see what's going on, and her face gives it away. Her eyes are teary, and she's smiling, but it isn't a big smile, and I know why. If Dad were here, this would be a really special night for him. Maybe one of the best nights of his whole life. Nick Jersey sits at the bottom of the stairs with his guitar. A guy with black-framed glasses takes out his harmonica and pulls a chair over to Nick, and the drummer brings his bongos. The bongo player calls out, "One, two, three, four," and the band launches into a song I know I've heard on the kitchen radio before.

"Oh," I murmur. I *have* heard Nick Jersey and the Hudson Canyon Band. In the kitchen, with my parents. They've danced around to this song, making pancakes and scrambled eggs. It's the kind of song that makes me feel a little nostalgic for something I don't even understand. The *old days* they're singing about are at the end of the 1900s, and I wasn't alive then. I don't know what *Coney Island* is, or what *penny loafers* are, but I know my eyes are getting teary, too, because this song reminds me of some really good days with Mom and Dad at the Brake Fast, and it reminds me that they had some really good days without me, too, a long time before I was born. It reminds me that today isn't one of Dad's good days. But it's all right *enough.* And after the song, and after the goodbyes and the cleaning up, Mom and I will take food up to Dad, and we'll just stick with him and love him. And that's all. I wipe a tear away with the heel of my hand.

The song is almost over, and I look around the dining room. All the plates are practically scraped clean, which I take as a compliment.

Hugh is sitting across from Denver's mom, and—oh my God. They're holding hands. They're holding hands! Hugh's eyes are closed, enjoying the song, and Denver's mom is smiling at him without him even knowing it.

I share a look with Denver, who raises his eyebrows and cocks his head toward his mom and Hugh. He gets out of his seat and sneaks over to me.

"Look, this is fine with me. My mom's had it hard and deserves any happiness she can find," he whispers. "But I don't want Tick Tick as a brother."

I have to slap a hand over my mouth so I don't burst out laughing. Denver sneaks back to his seat.

When the song is over, everyone in the dining room stands up and gives the band a standing ovation.

Mom clatters around the kitchen cleaning up and closing down.

"You need help?" I ask.

"You cooked," she says. "I'll clean."

"Is that how it's going to be every time I make dinner?" I ask. "Because seriously, I'll cook every night if it means no dishes!"

Mom shoos me out of the kitchen with her drying towel. "Go talk to your friends. The mechanic is coming first thing in the morning, and the band has to go as soon as the bus is fixed."

My heart kind of slumps. I'd almost forgotten that they're all going to leave in the morning. I'd almost forgotten that *Denver's* going to leave in the morning.

I find him in the dining room, sitting at a table with Hudgie, whose mom is talking to the band, more animated than I've ever seen her. Denver's clicking through photos on his camera screen. He looks up.

"Tacoma, you've got to look at these."

I sit down next to him, across from Hudgie. On the screen is a photo of Hugh's chickens, red and fat and beautiful. Denver clicks a button. The three of us look through our whole day in pictures—the tunnel, Tick Tick, the Oddities shop, Mount Rainier over the ocean of corn, me in the maze, yelling out to Hugh, Hudgie, or Calvin. There's a picture of me in the kitchen, stirring something in a bowl while peering into the jambalaya pot. In the photo, my hair is a mess and I've got some kind of cooking crud on my cheek—pumpkin pie filling, maybe. Or cheese sauce. I touch my cheek. The crud's still there. I scrape it off with my thumbnail.

"These are so good," I tell Denver. "I mean, you're a really good photographer, Denver."

Denver's cheeks turn kind of pink. "Thanks. It was a really good day for taking photos. I don't get a whole lot of those."

He nudges me with his shoulder. "It was a really good day in general, actually."

Warmth spills over me, and I feel really happy and tired and *good*. But I also feel like I'm going to cry.

"Actually—" Hudgie starts to say, but his voice breaks and it sounds like he's about to cry, too. "This was probably the best day of my life. Not to sound like a total doof, but." He sniffs. "It was."

"Mine too, Hudgie," I say. And I really think it was.

We all sit in silence for a long moment.

"I wish you didn't have to go," I say to Denver. "It's really weird to say this, because I just met you this morning, and Hudgie, I've known *you* most of my life, but we've never been friends. Not ever. I mean, I don't really *have* friends. Or I didn't before today. But now—"

"You're my friends, too," says Hudgie, wiping his nose on his sleeve. "Probably my only real friends."

Denver smiles a heartbreaking kind of smile that doesn't even have the tiniest hint of sarcasm around it. "I live on a bus with a bunch of middle-aged men and my mom. Generally, I don't do friends. But I can tell you with complete certainty that I do now."

The door jingles as a few members of the Hudson Canyon Band make their way out to sleep on the bus.

"It isn't smoking anymore," says Denver's mom, appearing by our table with Hugh. "Let's get some sleep out there, kid. Tacoma, that dinner was incredible. You've got real talent."

"Thanks." I grin. And then I notice that Hugh is carrying her tote bag.

“You get some good John Denver stories, Hugh?” I ask.

“The best,” says Hugh. “And from the best woman I’ve ever met in my life.”

“Oh dear,” says Denver.

“Oh wow,” I say.

“Let me walk you out?” Hugh asks Denver’s mom.

She beams up at him. “I hoped you would.”

Hugh pauses, then crouches down till he’s eye-level with Hudgie.

“It was a pleasure getting to know you today, Hudgie. I mean that. You’re welcome at the Grange anytime, okay?”

Hudgie blinks in surprise, and a grateful smile tugs on the corner of his mouth. “Thanks, Hugh. I promise I’ll never stomp your pumpkins again.”

Hugh nods. “Well, I’ll tell you what. You come on by after Halloween. That’s when I load the leftover pumpkins into the compost bin. You can stomp them as much as you like then.”

Hudgie’s face lights up like the sun. “Oh, man. I’d love that.”

“Thanks, Hugh,” I say. “For everything.”

Hugh winks and walks Denver’s mom to the door. They leave with a jingle, and with Hugh’s hand on Nan’s back. Denver’s face is so uncomfortable I can’t help laughing.

“Well, everything’s fun and games till Hugh steals your mom,” Denver says. His eyes are kind of twinkly.

“On the bright side, maybe you’ll get to visit a lot, if your mom’s dating Hugh,” says Hudgie hopefully.

Denver considers this. “You know what, Hudgie? You’re right. Maybe today wasn’t our last adventure. If the price I have to pay is Tick Tick, I guess it's not the worst thing in the world. But if he's in the wedding, I'm not going."

The three of us laugh until our ribs hurt. We laugh until the remaining band members trickle out into the chilly October night. We laugh until Hudgie's mom comes to collect him.

"See you again soon," Hudgie says to me and Denver.

"See you, Hudgie," I say.

"See you soon," says Denver.

Hudgie smiles at us both. Then his mom walks him out into the night, landing a kiss on top of his head right before the door closes behind them.

Mom comes out of the kitchen looking happy and tired.

"Almost bedtime, kiddo. Want to bring a piece of pie up to your dad?" Mom asks.

I sigh. "Yeah." I don't want to say goodnight, but I'm also bone-tired. Everything feels sore—my legs, my arms, my neck. And I want to see Dad.

"We're leaving pretty early tomorrow, so I'll say goodbye now," says Denver.

Goodbye. A truck stop is all about goodbyes. I say goodbye all the time to truckers heading across the country. I see some of them again, and some of them I don't. But I've never been this sad about a goodbye before.

"Goodbye, Denver," I say.

The door jingles.

"Denver Cass," calls Nan. "Bus. You've gotta get some sleep."

I blink away tears that are blurring my vision.

"It's not goodbye forever, I promise," says Denver. He pulls me into a hug. I bury my face in his bear sweater. "Okay, let's try not to cry on the cashmere."

I attempt a smile, but a fat tear runs down my cheek, and it dissolves me into kind of a sobbing mess.

"Relax, kids," calls Nan. "We're coming back for Thanksgiving." She grins. "I'm not about to let Hugh spend it on his own."

"Thanksgiving?" I pull away and shake Denver by the shoulders. "You're coming here for Thanksgiving! *Denver.* I just had the best idea. I'll make a giant turkey for everybody—my family and you and your mom and Hugh and the band and Hudgie and *his* mom—and you can help me! We'll have stuffing and mashed potatoes and sweet potato casserole and oh! That weird green bean casserole that is, like, inexplicably delicious. Pumpkin pie is kind of our specialty now, so obviously we'll make a few of those, and we'll have pecan pie and chocolate cream pie and maybe—"

"Denver Cass," Nan says again. "*Bed.*"

I let out a breath. "Wait. Do you have a piece of paper? Can I get your email address?"

Denver peels a napkin from the dispenser on our table and rips it in two. He pulls a pen out of his pocket and scribbles down his email address and his mom's phone number. Then he hands the pen to me. I write down my email, Mom's phone number, and my home address. "In case you're in, like, an old-fashioned mood," I say.

Denver folds the piece of napkin and puts it in his pocket. "You never know," he says. "Goodbye for now, Tacoma Jones."

"See you at Thanksgiving," I say, because that's a lot easier than saying goodbye.

I watch him leave with Nan. I watch as Mom locks the door behind him and turns out the dining room lights. I join her in the kitchen and take up the pie plate with the last piece of pie. Mom takes up three forks.

Mom and Dad's bedroom looks the same way it did this morning. Dad's lying in bed, his same old water glass on the nightstand.

"We brought you pie," I say softly.

"Tacoma made it. I brought us some forks so we can share," Mom says.

Dad nods weakly. He straightens out his mouth into not-quite-a-smile.

We climb into bed with him, one on either side. Dad tries to sit up. Mom adjusts the pillow for him.

"I'm sorry," he says. "It's hard to talk." He swallows.

There's a wall between me and my words. I can chip away at that wall and get a few words out, but it's a lot of work.

"We don't have to talk. Let's eat pie," I say. And I swear, I almost see a flicker of a real smile in him. It's deep in him, and it doesn't quite make it to his mouth, but it's there.

"*Diners, Drive-Ins and Dives*?" Mom asks, resting her face on Dad's shoulder.

"Sounds all right to me."

We stay like that until it's well past bedtime, watching Guy Fieri, listening to the rumbling of trucks along Route 202, eating pie together in bed, and it's all right *enough*.

CHAPTER 22

The second week of November is unusually cold. This is the beginning of what we call a La Niña winter in the Pacific Northwest. It means there'll be snow—maybe a lot of it. It means the roads will be a mess, because we don't have the resources for big snowfalls. It means we're going to host a lot more truckers in our parking lot overnight, when they close the pass through the Cascade Mountains and it's most dangerous to drive. It means things at the Brake Fast will be louder and warmer and cheerier than other winters, and I don't mind at all. La Niña years are my dad's favorites, too.

Mom and Dad confirmed that we're expecting Nick Jersey and the Hudson Canyon Band—and most importantly, Denver and his mom and Hugh—for Thanksgiving dinner, and Hudgie told me he and his mom are coming, too. I've already got shopping lists organized and recipes dog-eared in my cookbooks. I can't wait. Another day with Denver and Hudgie, and another dinner at the Brake Fast.

Actually, I've been making dinner every weekend, and it's been going so well. We've started getting a lot more traffic in here on Saturday nights, and my dad thinks it's because word's getting out about my dinners. Truckers talk. At this rate, when I've got my cross-country food truck someday, I'll already have a loyal clientele.

"Tacoma Jones, I've got some exciting mail for you!" Mom blows into the dining room with a stack of mail in one hand and a flat-ish brown package in the other. She drops it on the table in front of me.

The package is addressed to me, and it says it's from:

Denver Cass
A bus
Somewhere in the great state of Colorado

I rip the package open, and the contents nearly knock me off my chair. It's a cookbook for my collection! *Rocky Mountain Fry: The Colorado Culinary Experience.* There's a sticky note slapped onto the cover, in Denver's handwriting.

T,
Check out the recipe for Rocky Mountain Oysters. See you soon!
D

Mom looks over my shoulder. "Rocky Mountain Oysters? Those sound good."

I flip the book open and turn to page 134—Rocky Mountain Oysters.

I read the ingredients and dissolve into laughter.

"What?" Mom asks.

I push the book over to her. Her eyes scan the page. Then her face takes on kind of a green color. "I retract what I said about them sounding good. Let's never find out."

I can't stop laughing. Tears are coming out of my eyes, and Mom closes hers. Her shoulders start shaking.

"What's all this about?" asks Dad, coming from upstairs.

"Bull testicles," I say, at the same time Mom says, "Denver Cass."

We burst into a new fit of laughter and carry on like that—crying and shaking and laughing—until the front door jingles open and a trucker comes in and sits down.

"I'll get this one," I say, dabbing the corners of my eyes with the sleeve of my sweatshirt. I make my way over to him. "Morning, sir! Can I get you started with a cup of coffee?"

ACKNOWLEDGMENTS

Thank you, thank you to my husband, Zach, who reads my first drafts and tenth drafts with equal enthusiasm. Your support, love, and early edits are everything. Thank you to all three of my kids, Maddie, Simon, and Cecily, for being constant sources of inspiration, and thank you to all my children's teachers, paraprofessionals, aides, librarians, OTs, speech therapists, and office staff, for educating and caring for my kids every single weekday. This book was mostly written during those school hours.

Thank you to my phenomenal agent, Samantha Wekstein, who has been a perpetual champion for Tacoma *and* for me. I appreciate you so much.

Thank you to my wonderful editor, Courtney Stevenson! Working with you has been an absolute dream. And thank you to everyone at Quill Tree Books and HarperCollins Children's Books—I'm still pinching myself over here. I'm unbelievably lucky to have worked on this book with all of you.

Thank you to Becky Sosby for saying "Let's do it, Lute!" every single time I need a research trip buddy. You're just the best.

Thank you to Janet Scott, my dear friend and hunter of both typos and four-leaf clovers.

Thank you to Megan Lacera and Gaia Cornwall, whose wonderful edits and suggestions were critical to Tacoma's story.

Our biweekly chats have made my creative life so much richer, and I'm lucky to know you both.

Thank you to my critique group of a whole *decade* (happy anniversary to us!): Lenae Nofziger, Ann Strawn, Laura Barfield, and Barrett. I appreciate every edit and suggestion, and your support and friendship mean the world.

Thank you to Caralie, the therapist who changed my life and provided me with all the grounding exercises Tacoma uses in this book.

Thank you to Nancy for being willing to answer all my questions, and thank you to my friends and family for all your support. Thank you especially to Mom, whose invaluable support sometimes looks like childcare while I write.

Thank you to the heroes of music, food, and compassion who I snuck in throughout this book.